BROODING CITY

A BROODING CITY NOVEL

TOM SHUTT

Published by Red Eagle

Visit us at www.redeaglepublishing.com

ISBN: 978-1-7334810-0-7

Cover design by Mibl Art (www.miblart.com)

DEDICATION

The family of Tom Shutt dedicates this novel to his eternal memory, following his abrupt physical departure from this world at age 25. Thomas passed away peacefully from an unexplained sudden cardiac arrhythmia while working on a new novel, less than a year after landing on the *New York Times* Bestseller List. He is profoundly missed and infinitely loved.

The novel that you're currently holding includes updated cover art designed before his passing, but never released until now. Aside from that change, everything you're about to read is exactly what he wrote for you to enjoy.

Proceeds from all book sales go directly to the Thomas J. Shutt Memorial Foundation, a registered 501(c)(3) nonprofit dedicated to supporting the next generation of great storytellers through scholarships and grants. You can learn more about the foundation at www.thomasjshuttmemorialfoundation.org.

CONTENTS

ACKNOWLEDGMENTS

We would like to thank the international independent author community for so many things. Most importantly, for your friendship and support of Thomas as he established himself in his career as a young writer. Thomas spoke often of his friends around the world who shared his passion for creative storytelling, and he was so grateful to have each of you in his life. Thank you for giving him that sense of belonging.

To Derek Armstrong, Kylie Colter, Monica Corwin, Danielle Romero, Gwynn White, and so many others we've come to know through this tragedy, we truly do not have words to express our gratitude for how you rallied around our family in our darkest days. We love and appreciate each of you, and know that Thomas is so proud.

To the entire team at Mibl Art, especially Mark and Olivia, we can't thank you enough for bringing Thomas's design vision for his books to life. Your talents as designers are only exceeded by your compassion, patience and kindness as human beings. Thank you for being who you are.

Finally, we would like to acknowledge you, the reader. Every time you read Thomas's words and talk about his books with your family and friends, you contribute to keeping his legacy alive. We are eternally grateful for that.

CHAPTER ONE

THE TABBY HAD a complete and utter disregard for the sanctity of the crime scene.

It avoided the still-damp bloodstains closest to the body, but its tail flicked and papers fell as it jumped to the desk and then the wardrobe, from the top of which it watched the entire room through half-closed eyes.

A steady rain muted the light of the ever-burning streetlamps, its pitter-patter a comforting background noise that drowned out the sounds of the city. It was as if a shade had fallen around the ramshackle apartment.

The corpse reclined on a large, brown leather sofa facing a wall-sized plasma screen. Hooked up to the television were a set of studio-performance stereos and one of the latest generation gaming consoles, an unassuming black box with only a single cable connecting to the screen. A controller lay on the floor by the dead man's feet. His clothes were thoroughly soaked through with red, and a shallow pool of blood had collected in the seat of the leather cushion.

Detective Brennan flashed his badge to the officer standing guard and carefully ducked beneath the yellow tape that blocked the doorway, balancing two brown cups in one oversized hand as he entered. He replaced the badge in his jacket while he looked over the crime scene, casting a critical eye at the body and frowning at the perched cat. He tried to ignore the strong metallic odor that hung in the air, but it left a coppery taste in his mouth. His partner of several months, Noel Bishop, beckoned him to join her in the kitchen.

"Arthur, over here," she said.

He nodded in greeting. "Bishop," he said, handing her one of the coffees. At an easy six-five, Brennan towered over her by nearly a foot.

She took a long sip from her cup and sighed, the tension visibly easing out of her as she drank. It had been a long week for both of them, and Brennan realized that she had probably been on the verge of sleep when the call dragged her from home.

Brennan drank from his own cup and rolled his shoulders. Several joints popped in place. "What do we have here?" he asked.

"Zachariah Nettle. Body was found about an hour

ago by the landlord, who was responding to a noise complaint from the tenant downstairs. Time of death is placed at around 10 p.m. No sign of forced entry."

"So he knew the person, or someone sneaked in." Brennan rubbed at his scalp. "That doesn't exactly narrow it down."

"He was sitting down when it happened," Bishop said, "and the television was still blaring loud when we got here. It's possible he never heard it coming."

"All right, then I'm leaning toward a sneak. And he was playing a video game?"

"Right."

"Imagine that would be difficult without eyes." Brennan frowned and walked toward the body. The tabby hissed from atop the wardrobe as he passed. He crouched in front of the corpse; it smelled worse from up close. He looked at the pale face of the late Zachariah Nettle. Rivulets of dried blood trailed from the empty eye sockets. There was some kind of irritation around the dark, sunken holes, and the mouth was agape in a frozen scream. Noel was speaking from somewhere behind him.

"Multiple stab wounds to the chest punctured the heart and both lungs," she said.

"So why take the eyes afterward?"

"Maybe the killer has a thing for collecting trophies," Bishop suggested. "A knife wouldn't cause that kind of irritation around the eyes unless it was coated with something."

"Did the forensics team find anything?"

"Came up empty on the eyes." She grimaced at her choice of words. "They took swabs from the chest wounds back to the lab, just to be sure."

Brennan looked around the small apartment. The stereo systems, the gaming console, the furniture, even the kitchen appliances—they didn't feel right. It meant something, he was sure of it.

When he was younger, setting off on his own without help from his family, his apartment had been terribly rundown. He could barely afford to live in the city, and it was only once his parents had passed away that he had lived in anything more than a glorified closet. His apartment now wasn't exactly a palace, but it was nothing to sneeze at. And it had taken him years and some amount of chance to reach that point.

"Bishop, how old was our victim?" he asked.

"Twenty-four," she supplied. "Why?"

"Because," he said, gesturing to everything in the room, "I don't think our victim bought all of this on his own." As he said it, he felt in his bones that he was right.

And everything in this apartment felt very, very wrong.

CHAPTER TWO

THE TOWER LOOMED OMINOUSLY in the darkness.

Jeremy Scott crouched low, peering from the tall grass just beyond the old fort's crumbling outer wall. There was no other term for the monument that stood before him. Illuminated intermittently by the moon peeking through the clouds, the Tower appeared black against the already dark backdrop of the mountains behind it. The range of peaks surrounded the entirety of his father's valley. The central, rounded structure literally towered over the rest of the fort's meager surviving structures.

He hissed in discomfort as one of the long blades of switchgrass sliced a fine cut along his cheek. Kneeling as he was, his face was in the thick of the slender, dangerous plants. He had worn long sleeves and jeans for the express purpose of pushing the grass away, but he had moved too suddenly without thinking.

He took careful strides through the grass as he made his way toward the fort. It was the closest he had ever been, only ever seeing faint glimpses of it from the trail as he passed by with his father. His birthday had been last week, though, and this was his personal celebration.

In daylight, the fort might have been less intimidating. As it was, the rusted iron bars that rimmed the decrepit entrance looked like grasping metal claws in the moonlight, an image which did little to put Jeremy's worries to rest. He took a deep breath and grasped one of the metal bars, using it for leverage as he pulled himself up from the ditch that surrounded the fort.

Small rocks crunched beneath his feet as he entered. He squinted to see in the dim glow from the moon; husks of low, squat buildings greeted him from the shadows. The nearest one looked like an old storage shed, with fragments of broken pots and tools lying scattered on the ground. One of its large, wooden support beams had long since fallen, and the structure looked ready to collapse beneath its own weight.

A gust of wind suddenly rose from the west, and Jeremy shied away, covering his eyes from the dirt that swirled in the air. A booming crack resounded from one of the shed's other support beams, and the stone wall closest to him gave way with a grinding groan of protest. Jeremy jumped away just as the entire building caved in. Dust and dirt threatened to suffocate him, and he coughed severely as he moved away from the cloud that slowly drifted outward from the rubble.

That, he thought, *was awesome.*

It was a shame nobody had been around to see his nimble dive away from the collapsing shed. Little enough happened in the valley that Jeremy took every opportunity to seek excitement. Their ranch was fine for a weekend getaway from the city, but in the case of staying for the entire summer, he very quickly ran out of things to do indoors. While his sister could content herself with imaginary friends and playdates by the pond, Jeremy needed more activity. It was the very reason that he was wandering around in the valley after dark, very much against his parents' wishes.

A large figure on horseback was silhouetted against the imposing Tower, and a broken sword was held aloft toward the starry sky. Jeremy slowly approached the stone soldier, admiring the statue even as he paced around it from a wary distance. From hooves to hilt, the statue was nearly fifteen feet tall, and a low, empty basin encircled it. The blade of the sword had broken off and lay in stone shards beneath the horse's raised forelegs. There was a plaque attached to the statue, but it would have been too dark to read even if the words hadn't been worn away by the elements.

A soft rain began to fall. Jeremy found it harder to see as the moon and stars were obscured by incoming clouds. He looked up wistfully at the Tower; this was the closest he had ever been, and now a fast and fierce storm was coming into the valley. If he did not turn back now, there was a good chance that he would be caught in the worst part of the deluge.

Reluctantly, he turned away from the Tower and jogged to the fort's entrance. The ditch that surrounded the fort was now lined with a thin layer of mud at the bottom, and Jeremy realized that it would soon be a full-on moat—without a drawbridge to cross—once the rain started falling in earnest. He slid down the dirt wall and scrambled up the far embankment, spurred on faster as the raindrops grew bigger and more frequent.

Switchgrass tugged at his long sleeves and jeans as he rushed to beat the storm home.

CHAPTER THREE

"JESUS CHRIST."

Bishop bridled. "Brennan, little respect, okay?"

"Jesús Cristo."

"You're an asshole."

"Now who's cursing?"

The weekend had been full of nothing but dead-ends and false leads, and the stress was getting to Brennan. The rain had persisted all throughout, lingering until dawn broke on Monday, clouds parting to reveal a warming early sun hanging low under an azure sky. Of course, the view would have been better from one of the corner offices. The police station had a generally open floor plan, with little regard for the detectives' personal space. The only divider was a low wall of opaque glass and plaster which separated the working detectives and the hallway along which offices and the elevator were situated. On the other side of the desk farm were separate rooms for interviews and observations.

Ordinarily, Bishop was able to handle a lot more verbal sparring with Brennan, or at least hid her frustration better. Working in the boys' club that was the Odols Police Department, she had to be thick-skinned to survive. But Brennan recognized that going in on her religion was a low blow; he was backing off just as footsteps approached from the elevator.

Sam McCarthy, a former detective turned private investigator, sauntered into the desk farm at exactly the wrong moment. Lean of build and crowned with a short crop of curly hair, the sharp-tongued redhead put the "ass" in "sass", and his horribly failed relationship with Noel Bishop had in no way bettered her view of him.

"Morning, Detective," he said cheerily to Brennan before turning to Bishop. "And good morning to you, too, Detect*ess*."

Her glare would have warded off a cobra, but Sam's grin remained intact. "I've already had too much masculine bullshit to deal with today," she scowled. "Why are you here?"

"Language, please," Sam said, feigning shock.

"I know, right? She's on a roll with that today," Brennan remarked. Bishop sent him a dark glare.

Sam leaned a casual hand against her desk. "Can't a fellow just be courteous and drop by to see his friends at work?"

"If we were friends, I could believe that, but since we're n—"

"I can't have other friends in the department? Arthur here, of course, and then there's the Chief…" He started listing off names, counting one on each finger and cycling through both hands before starting over. "And Wallace, down in the morgue…"

Brennan sighed. "All right, stop antagonizing her, Sam. Were you able to find what I asked for?"

Sam smirked and turned his back on Bishop, who was quickly turning red in the face. The wooden armrests of her chair groaned beneath her white-knuckled grip. "Have I ever failed you?" He dropped a thin manila folder onto Brennan's lap and casually availed himself of the last stale donut from the box on a nearby desk. He took one bite and scowled, then tossed it clear across the room. It landed in the trash bin with a smooth swish of plastic.

Brennan, meanwhile, looked through the folder. It wasn't much, but Sam had compiled some useful information on Zachariah Nettle during the weekend. He reached for the donut box only to find empty air, and his stomach gave a loud grumble of protest.

"Detective?"

"Hmm?" Brennan looked up and caught Sam's expectant eyes. "You'll receive payment the usual way."

"I always insist on cash, Arthur, you know that."

"And I always pay by online deposit. Now get out of here before Bishop trades in that grip on her chair for one on your neck."

Sam glanced back at Bishop, whose poisonous glare had lost none of its bite, and grinned madly. "I miss our little tête-à-têtes, Noel," he said. "Perhaps we should split a bottle of Chardonnay and smooth things over."

"Get out."

"Ah, I remember now, you're a rosé sort of girl. We'll talk!" He called out that last part as he disappeared behind the partition. A moment later, they heard a ding as the elevator was called for. Bishop turned to level a stare at Brennan. Though it no longer held the vast arctic iciness she held in reserve for Sam, there was still a measure of anger behind those eyes.

"How are you still friends with that pig?"

"He's not a pig, remember? He left the force years ago."

She sighed wearily. "God, you two are impossible."

"Hey, I'd appreciate it if you didn't take His name is vain. It's a personal kind of thing for me, you know?"

Bishop's eyes became harsh slits.

Brennan cleared his throat. "How about we get some breakfast?"

The proposition came unexpectedly, and for a moment Bishop's anger subsided. "Breakfast?"

"Yeah, it's something I do most days. Silly little thing, food, but my body seems to like it." The moment was punctuated by another grumbling of his stomach, louder than the first.

"I know what it is," she said evenly. "But your impersonation of Sam is improving. For a moment, I thought he hadn't even left."

Brennan stood, picking up the folder Sam had given him. "So your answer is…?"

Bishop sighed. "Yeah, I'm coming. I'll never say no to a free meal."

He raised an eyebrow. "Who said I was paying?"

CHAPTER FOUR

"WHERE DID YOU go on Friday?"

Ellie's voice startled Jeremy out of his daydreaming. It had rained for the better part of the past two days, and he was going stir-crazy in the house with only his kid sister around as company. She was on the cusp of being a teenager, yet Ellie still acted like a girl half her age. It could be cute and endearing sometimes, but only in small doses.

Everything in moderation.

Jeremy rubbed at his eyes. "What do you mean?"

"Don't play stupid," she said, small hands on her hips. "You snuck out after Mom fell asleep. Where did you run off to?"

"I have no idea what you're talking about, and you can't prove otherwise."

Ellie bit her lower lip and frowned at him. "I'm

almost thirteen," she said proudly. "You don't have to treat me like a child."

Ah, so today she's being mature. I wonder how long that will last. Jeremy sighed. "I'm not trying to patronize you. I just don't want you tattling on me again to Mom or Dad."

She moved a finger across her chest. "Cross my heart and hope to die."

"Stick a needle in your eye?"

"Hmm." She considered it for a long moment. "No, not that far. I hate needles."

Jeremy weighed his options. There was always the risk that Ellie would break her promise and run her mouth off like she usually did. However, if he kept her in the dark, she could simply run to their father and say that Jeremy was keeping a secret from her. An indirect tattle, but with the same end result. Telling her outright at least had the added benefit of some peace and quiet from her incessant questioning.

"I went to the Tower."

Ellie wrinkled her nose. "That place is dirty and old. Why would you want to go there?"

Because being cooped up in here with you is driving me crazy. "It's the coolest thing we've seen since coming out here," he said instead. "Aren't you the least bit curious about what's out there?"

"Mom said we're supposed to stay close to the

house." She reported the cardinal rule with an adopted voice of authority. It was a voice he had heard before, and one which signaled that she might flip on her vow of secrecy.

"Look at me," Jeremy said. "Do I look hurt? Everything is fine, I promise."

She still appeared unconvinced.

Jeremy frowned and looked directly into her eyes. "If I promise not to go back there, will you promise not to tell Mom and Dad?"

Ellie chewed her lip for a few seconds before nodding.

"I promise to stay away from the Tower," he said solemnly. He felt bad lying to his sister, but it was the only way to make her keep quiet. Besides, he was still mostly being honest with her. The Tower wasn't dangerous, and it *was* the most interesting thing they had seen in the valley.

"Good," Ellie said, nodding again. "Do you know when Mom is getting back today?"

"No idea."

Even though the two of them were home for the summer, their parents still had busy work schedules that kept them in Odols. While his mother was able to return to the valley ranch most nights—whenever she wasn't staying late to host some fundraiser she'd organized—Jeremy's father typically stayed in their large city apartment except for the odd weekend visit. This hadn't been one of those weekends.

Ellie hid a yawn behind her hand and stood unsteadily, her long, black hair wafting silkily in her wake. "I'm going to go take a nap."

"Don't let the Sleepers get you," Jeremy teased, a grin tugging at his lips.

In an instant, Ellie became her much younger self. "I've been a good girl," she said, her voice childish and sweet. "They won't come for me."

"Good girls keep promises."

She nodded sleepily. "Cross my heart," she repeated, "and hope to die."

Jeremy watched her until she rounded the corner, then listened attentively. Once he heard her door shut, he sprung up from his seat by the window and retrieved a small pack that he had secreted away beneath the cushion. Inside was enough food for the trip to and from the Tower, plus an umbrella, in case the rain decided to start again. He wrote a note to Ellie, telling her that he had gone to roam around the orchards and read, and left it on the kitchen table for her to find.

Jeremy opened the door and squinted. The clouds had parted, and sunlight shone from a light-blue sky above. His mood was greatly improved by the change in weather, and he was upbeat about returning to the

Tower during the full light of day. He set off boldly, eager to start the hike that would take several hours, and he followed the southward trail away from the ranch.

Chapter Five

DRIVING IN THE city was never enjoyable.

Traffic was a nightmare, any given hour of the day. Taxis were belligerent, swerving madly in and out of spaces just wide enough to squeeze by if they suspended any sense of self-preservation. Pedestrians walked out in the street whenever they liked, crosswalk or not, and the sidewalks were more like temporary auxiliary lanes for cars.

The OST was hardly a better option. Odols Shuttle Transit wound in a wagon wheel circuit beneath the city, leading to all the different sectors in the fastest way possible. It was the preferred mode of transportation for many in the city, which was precisely why it had become as dirty and crowded as the streets above.

Brennan, having worked in the city for years, was

aware of all this. Most of his social life took place within one shuttle stop of the police headquarters. He lived in an apartment less than a block from the station, and the diner that he and Detective Bishop were now sitting in was one of his local favorites. The walk was a short but healthy addition to the day.

Especially for an aging detective subsisting on stale donuts and coffee.

The Box Car Diner had the typical morning crowd. Coffee drinkers at the counter chatting up the head waitress. A pair of construction workers grabbing a quick breakfast before heading to their job site. There was a family of four in the corner. The children eagerly scribbled on the backs of their menus with crayons.

Bishop was still irritated from before, though the walk had released some of her tension. Her need for food was also a mitigating factor, and Brennan knew it would soon be a non-issue. It was hard to be angry on a full stomach.

"How are you doing?"

Bishop looked up at him with tired eyes. "How do you mean?"

"I mean with everything that happened between you and Sam."

"Sam and I aren't anything anymore. I just wish he'd stay out of my life."

"He's my friend, Noel." Brennan sighed. "Look,

I'm not asking you two to get back together—"

"Lord knows that'll never happen," Bishop muttered.

"—but there must be some way you can bury the hatchet. Call a truce. What happened, happened, and we can't go back and change it."

"Nobody's asking you to do anything, Brennan. You aren't a part of this."

He held his hands up. "Sorry, poor choice of words. *You* can't change the past, is what I'm saying. But he's my friend, and he used to mean something to you, too. And we both know he's damn good at his job."

"I'm damn good at *my* job, too," she said, her voice hard. "And I don't appreciate you treating me the same way he does. You're my partner, Brennan. We're supposed to trust each other, but that's hard to do when you act like a jackass."

"Bishop," he said, stunned. "I was just joking, I didn't mean—"

"What was in that folder he gave you?"

"Don't change the subject."

Bishop shifted and crossed her arms, her eyes resolute. "Well, your jokes aren't funny, and I don't want to talk about it, so we might as well work the case. What did he find out?"

Brennan looked at her for a moment, his own eyes

hard. A few years his senior, Noel was a tough nut to crack. She was resilient, but some wounds took more time to heal, and adultery was one hell of a wound. Nothing he could say right then would sway her, and he knew that particular conversation was over. For now.

He took the manila folder from the seat and opened it on the table so Bishop could read. Her eyes scanned each page as she cycled through them, picking out relevant details.

"You had him look into Zachariah's financial history? Why? We know what he makes, he's just a part-time pharmacist."

"Right," Brennan said. "But did you look at where he was living? He had some things even I couldn't afford."

Bishop raised an eyebrow. "We don't make much."

"True enough. This kid is fresh out of college, though. He should be worrying about student loans and making enough money just to keep the heat on."

"The neighborhood was pretty bad. Maybe he took a cheap home in exchange for having his luxuries inside?"

"That could—"

Their food arrived, and Brennan pushed the folder toward the window so the plates could be set down. Sausage links, hash browns, two buttermilk biscuits, a Belgian waffle, and a glass of O.J. for Brennan. Coffee and a plate of "short stack" pancakes were placed before Bishop. Brennan thought of making a height joke, but wisely reconsidered.

"That could be true," he continued, cutting into his food. "What does it say about relatives?"

"Relatives?"

"He could be a trust fund baby," he said, shoving a piece of sausage into his mouth.

"Your parents secretly run a trust fund, don't they?" Bishop asked jokingly. She took a bite of her pancakes as she reached for the folder.

"Did everything come out all right here?" asked the waitress, suddenly reappearing. Brennan gave her what he meant to be an appreciative nod. "Great! I'll check back with you in a bit."

Papers rustled in Bishop's hands as she looked past Zachariah's financials and into his family history. "Says here that his parents are both living in Michigan, some small town in the middle of nowhere. They haven't had contact in years, so it's doubtful they're the ones supporting him."

Brennan grunted. It was puzzling, but it was also a dead end. "Let's put that aside for now," he said. "The motive: what was it? Cut a man up like that, that's personal. Bad blood between Nettle and our killer, that's for sure."

"He didn't even have time to stand," Bishop added. "The killer planned this out."

They both sat chewing their food noiselessly, thinking of the implications. It could have been a relationship gone wrong, like Bishop and McCarthy's, with the girlfriend turning into some sort of femme fatale. Another possibility was that Zachariah had somehow gotten himself into trouble, maybe borrowed money from the wrong people to pay off his loans and couldn't repay those debts. He did live in a rough neighborhood, after all. Or maybe they were completely off-base and it was a robbery gone wrong. The fact that Nettle had been caught off guard could just be a coincidence. The kinds of toys Zachariah had kept in that apartment were worth a small fortune. But none of them had gone missing, so—

"Might I interest either of you in some coffee?" asked a sweet voice. The waitress had returned.

Without raising an eye or turning her head, Bishop casually reached up and adjusted the strap of her shoulder holster. The butt of her gun just barely showed through the unzipped opening in her jacket. There was nothing overtly threatening in the gesture, but the waitress visibly gulped and took a step back.

"The bill is ready whenever you need it," she said hesitantly. She backed away quickly. "Thanks for coming in."

"Don't you think that was a little cruel?" Brennan asked.

"No harm done," Bishop murmured into her coffee. She looked toward the retreating waitress and smiled. It looked more like she was baring her teeth.

"You're insane," he told her, chuckling.

"We all have our flaws. So I've been thinking—and don't you dare say 'That's a nice change' or I will brain you," she threatened as Brennan opened his mouth. "I've been thinking that maybe someone knew who would want to hurt Nettle. His parents are estranged, but somebody who worked with him at the pharmacy could know something."

Brennan nodded. "Good thinking. Need me to come along?"

"No, I can handle it." She looked up at Brennan, taking in his lined face and sunken eyes. "Maybe you should head back home, get a few hours of sleep," she suggested. "You look like death."

"Death wished it looked this good." Brennan grinned, standing from the table.

"Oh, shut up. Go get the bill from our waitress." She smiled fiercely. "I think I've frightened her."

Chapter Six

Jeremy regretted not bringing a hat.

The storm clouds were a distant memory, and the sun beat down mercilessly upon his head. The blond atop his head reflected some of the light, and he was certainly better off than Ellie would have been with her curtains of raven-black hair, but his cheeks felt hot and his mouth had dried up entirely.

He had forgotten to change into pants before setting out for the Tower. While he was thankful for the breeze that blew against his bare legs, each step through the switchgrass left long, thin scratches on the exposed skin. Now, in addition to the accumulating cuts, Jeremy had to contend with impending dehydration.

The walk was longer than he'd realized, and he arrived at the Tower later than he would have liked. He jumped into and out of the moat with relative ease, his shoes breaking through the crust of dried mud at the bottom. He was grateful for the cool shelter provided by the shadowy interior of the largest building the fort had to offer. His heart pounded in his ears as he looked around the Tower from the inside for the first time.

The doorway opened into a large, circular chamber. As his eyes adjusted, Jeremy noticed that light actually filtered down into the room through the broken ceiling above. Dominating the center of the room was a massive stone table, square and imposing. It was a solid slab that merged seamlessly with the ground, as if it and the Tower had been hewn from the rock of the mountain itself.

Along one edge of the room was a short series of steps, also solid stone, which seemed to end abruptly as they met the wall. Jeremy walked closer and felt against the wall, looking for a pressure plate or hidden mechanism that might open a secret door, but his fingers only met cold, smooth stone. He flattened his palms against the wall and leaned his whole body into it, but the wall was unyielding. If there was a door, he couldn't open it.

He turned away, dejected, and noticed a strange series of deep, rectangular furrows that ascended a narrow strip of the wall. It took him a moment to recognize that the width and spacing formed a ladder leading up to the next floor. He crossed the room to it. His fingers fit easily in the smooth, regular openings made for a man's hands, and he climbed up and onto the most curious platform he had ever seen.

The light below had not, as he had thought, been filtering through breaks in the floor. The openings looked as regularly spaced and carved as the ladder had been and, taken altogether, the floor resembled a bicycle wheel, with a solid circular center. The ladder emerged between two of the wheel's spokes.

At the end of each spoke was a tall, curved window, five in total, though he didn't remember seeing the windows from outside. Each window had an embedded shape of stained glass, each one a unique image pulled from nature. Otherwise, the room was empty.

A light tremor passed through the stone, almost undetectable. Jeremy briefly considered leaving, worried that this building might come down around him as the other had a few days before, but the shaking stopped almost as soon as he felt it.

Jeremy tiptoed along his spoke until he had reached the center, and there he crouched, one knee resting against the stone. The building was old, older than old, and he couldn't be sure that this floor was as secure as it seemed. His shins were caked with dust as he kneeled.

Patiently, he waited, and minutes crept by with nothing happening. The stone didn't shift or crumble beneath him; nothing extraordinary unfolded. He sighed out a breath of relief. And disappointment.

What was I expecting?

"I should have climbed back down the ladder," he said to no one, shaking his head. "Stupid."

He stood again, feeling slightly foolish, and started walking back to the stone-etched ladder when a glimmer of light flashed in the corner of his eye. He glanced around, caught it again in his other eye, and turned to squarely face one of the windows—its stained-glass imprint looked like a puddle surrounded by sticks. Through the clear glass around it, light shimmered off something in the distance, and as he approached he could make out a ring of trees around a shimmering lake that looked almost black from so far away.

Something pulled at the edge of his awareness, grabbing for his attention, but he waved it off. It was almost mid-afternoon, and he could still make it home before sundown if he left now. Still, he could look out the other windows, just once, before he started the long walk home. He returned to the center and chose the next spoke to the right. Clockwise, he went to each window, and he saw in turn an orchard of fuzzy peach trees, a huge collection of flowers, and the familiar wild, open fields of the valley.

He walked confidently along the final spoke and looked out into a veritable blizzard of white flower petals. The ground was completely covered in them, and a flurry of petals danced in the wind, obscuring much of the view.

No, he thought, that's...snow. There was snow, right here before his eyes.

He took a step back. This was summer; there was no snow in the valley.

Another step and, unaware of his surroundings, Jeremy's foot slipped over the edge of the spoke and robbed him of his balance. He had enough time to realize that his orchards had pears, not peaches, before slamming his head against a neighboring spoke and plummeting to the stone floor below.

CHAPTER SEVEN

BRENNAN'S APARTMENT WAS furnished for comfort and function, rather than fashion.

The living room served as an entry point, housing a single couch, a reclining chair, and an unimpressive television set. On either side of the television stood bookshelves crammed with an assortment of well-thumbed titles that spent as much time in his hands as on the shelf. On the opposite wall was the door to his bedroom and adjoining bath.

He knew he should retire to the bedroom and at least try to sleep, just as he knew it was a useless endeavor. It wasn't that he wouldn't rest until the case was solved. Truth be told, he ached in his bones and would have given anything for twenty-four hours straight of safe, solid sleep. But he knew better.

The fact was that he hadn't slept more than a

couple spare hours on any given night in *years*. It had aged him before his time, and wearied lines now lay heavily on his once-young face. Sleep was a luxury that he could no longer afford.

No, sleep wasn't an option, so he threw himself into the habit he'd followed for years: calm, calculated detective work. He would take the frustration he carried with him and throw it into his work, chasing murderers as if they were the ones who personally robbed him of his rest. It wasn't an easy job, but it was safer than sleep.

He spent the day reviewing Sam's files. They knew the pharmacist, Zachariah Nettle, had been living beyond his means, though there was no explanation yet of how. The murder weapon, a knife, was easily concealable. There were no signs of forced entry, which indicated that Zachariah knew whoever had killed him. He didn't really buy the idea that this was a random attack. Why sneak in through the window, murder Nettle, and then leave all the valuables? The luxurious lifestyle and the violently personal nature of the murder were linked somehow.

So he looked over the pages again and again, not certain of what he was searching for, yet certain that there was *something*. He pored over Sam's financial history on Zachariah Nettle, but there was no record of supplemental income from either the parents or any second job.

He rubbed his hand over his eyes, willing himself to stay awake, but his eyes were heavy and he was losing focus. When his phone rang, he jolted in his seat. "Yeah?"

"Um, Uncle Arty?" It took Brennan a moment to recognize the voice on the other end.

"Greg? What's up? Is everything all right with your mother?"

"That's why I'm calling," he said.

His nephew sounded on edge, and Brennan sat up a little straighter. "What's wrong?"

"She's having one of her fits, it's really bad. I don't know if I can handle her this time. Can you help me? I think she might need to see a doctor."

A weight dropped in Brennan's gut. He knew what they would be told if she was taken to the hospital in her condition.

"Do you think you can come over?" his nephew asked plaintively.

"Yeah, Greg, just keep her calm until I get there." He grabbed his jacket and was halfway through the door. "I'll be over in ten minutes."

CHAPTER EIGHT

THE FIRST SENSATION he had was of pain.

It felt as if someone were going to work on the inside of his skull with a sledgehammer. His shoulders were stiff, and small flares of pain burned along the left side of his body as he struggled against the heavy sheets that were wrapped around him. Scrapes and bruises called out their existence to him as he slowly regained consciousness.

He hadn't yet opened his eyes, but his other senses compensated. He felt a dry heat against his face and heard the crackling of a well-fed fire, and he knew he was back in his bedroom at the ranch house. Only one ear seemed to be hearing properly, though. His lips were cracked, and his throat yearned for water. He heard a low growl and realized it had come from his stomach.

Jeremy opened his eyes and tried to rise in bed, but the simple sheets proved too much for his feeble strength. The fire continued to crackle as he lay there, though he couldn't manage to fall back asleep. He was too painfully aware of the aches in his body.

"You're back with us," remarked an unfamiliar female voice.

Someone shifted by the door, and footsteps rapidly approached the bed. "Jeremy?" That was undoubtedly his mother's voice.

He hadn't realized there were other people in the room until just then. Jeremy again struggled to rise, and this time succeeded in gaining a more upright sitting position, his back leaning against several pillows. In addition to an unfamiliar Asian woman and his mother, Jeremy noted with surprise that his father, Nathaniel Scott, stood by the fire, his face half lit by the flickering orange light. His arms were lightly wrapped in bandages and he held them crossed against his chest.

"Dad," he said uncertainly.

The strange woman gently placed a hand on Jeremy's head. "Don't overexert yourself." She felt for his temperature and evidently found it acceptable. "My name is Dr. Kai," she said, taking a stethoscope from around her neck. She placed it over his heart as she asked, "Can you tell me where you are?"

Jeremy's mind was too fragged to come up with a

clever response. "I'm at home," he told her directly.

Dr. Kai nodded. She replaced the stethoscope and took out a short, thin flashlight, no wider than a pencil. "I want you to follow the light with only your eyes." He followed the light as she moved it in straight lines, this way and that. "Do you remember what happened?"

"I was—" Jeremy faltered for a moment. The memory came to him, but it seemed an absurd fabrication now. Of course there was no snow. "I fell," he said simply.

"You remember," she said, her voice pleased. "That's good. I don't see any signs of a concussion, which is fortunate." Her dark eyes met Jeremy's for a moment before she looked away. If there was something significant in that glance, he didn't know what it was.

He raised an uneasy hand and felt a long strip of gauze wrapped around his head over a thick bandage. "I'm not in a hospital," he said numbly.

"Dr. Kai works with me," his father said, speaking for the first time. His gray eyes turned from the fire to look at Jeremy, and then at the doctor. "You can go," he told her.

Dr. Kai nodded. "If anything else happens, or his condition worsens, you *will* need to take him to a hospital," she warned him.

Nathaniel nodded. "I understand, thank you." He opened the door for Dr. Kai, who gathered her supplies and left quickly and silently. A prolonged, awkward silence reigned. There was only the crackling of the fire to fill the room with sound until they heard the engine of the doctor's car come to life and fade as she drove away.

"Anna," his father said quietly.

"He just woke up." Annabelle spoke firmly, dismissively, then turned to face her son.

Jeremy took note of the wearied look in her eyes. The skin of her face was anchored less tightly to her high cheekbones than it might have been a few years ago, and her blonde hair had lost its luster, but the loving smile she gave him had remained unchanged throughout his life. It was a comfort, even in the darkest of times.

"Jay," she said softly. "How are you feeling?"

"I'm fine," Jeremy said, swallowing hard. Honestly, his throat was parched, and he cringed to think of what he would see if he looked in the full-length standing mirror across the room.

"Do you need me to bring you anything?" his mother asked. "Some more blankets?"

Between the fire and the heavy covers, he was already sweating. "A glass of water?" he suggested.

She nodded, rising fluidly from her chair. "I'll be

right back."

Jeremy's father waited for her to disappear before he left his post near the fire and walked slowly to the bed, all leonine grace and poise. He wasn't terribly tall or broad in the shoulders, but he carried a certain sense of purpose that gave him an air of subtle, unshakeable power. Nathaniel replaced Jeremy's mother on the stool by his bed and looked into his eyes. He sat there patiently, eyes never wavering. "You were playing in the ruins," he said finally. It wasn't a question.

"How did you know?"

His father's patient stare gave him all the answer he needed.

Jeremy's heart fell. "Ellie told you," he concluded.

Nathaniel nodded. "You shouldn't have left her here alone," he said. His voice was harsh, his words reproachful.

Jeremy cowered beneath the gaze of his father's gray eyes as his mother returned with a glass of water. "Thanks," he mumbled, taking a sip.

Annabelle looked between Jeremy and his father, and they stared back at her in silence. With a sigh, his mother left the room again, closing the door behind her.

"I didn't mean to leave Ellie alone," Jeremy blurted out. "I meant to be home before Mom showed up, I swear."

His father shook his head. "You aren't in trouble because you were caught," he said. "You're in trouble because you did the wrong thing. It's never safe to go off on your own, *especially* when your mother and I aren't around." His face softened for a moment. "And you know how lonely your sister gets without your company."

Jeremy tried to shrug, but the movement hurt his shoulder. "I tried to hang out with her yesterday, but she wanted to be alone."

"Really?" His father sounded skeptical. "That's not like Eloise."

"I don't know what it is about this place," Jeremy said, referring to the valley. "She seems to love it, but at the same time I feel like she's a different person here."

"Regardless of how your sister is acting," his father said, "family still comes first."

Jeremy let out a harsh laugh. "When did *that* become your motto?"

He wished he could bite back the words as soon as he said them. Anger flashed across his father's eyes like a bolt of lightning, sparking from nothing before disappearing. If he hadn't been watching, Jeremy might have missed it altogether.

His father sighed, his face suddenly much more haggard than Jeremy was used to seeing. "I'm sorry,

Jeremy," he said, his eyes taking on a quality that was as rare as Bigfoot. They looked almost warm. Friendly, even. "Living with me, dealing with the effects of my work schedule—I know that it must have been difficult for you. I've always been one step too far away from you kids for my comfort, but that's just the nature of the industry. Business is a beast, and I'm in its clutches." He placed a long, slender hand on top of Jeremy's, and he smiled. "But I am trying the best I can to be your father."

Jeremy tried to respond, but he was suddenly gripped with an overwhelming sense of vertigo. His eyes danced with light as the world around him was swapped out, piece by piece. Gone were his desk and schoolbooks, the mirror and the fireplace, and even his father.

In place of his bedroom was a large office of some sort. A long, oval table of sturdy wood ran the length of the center of the room, and men and women in smart business suits sat along both sides. An entire wall of the room was made of plate-glass windows, and the office had an incredible view of Odols. The sun was setting, silhouetting the city's skyline in inky black contrast to its vibrant red and orange and purple.

Jeremy stood by one of the other walls, and every member of the meeting had their eyes trained on him as he spoke. His voice was confident and powerful, and his arms accompanied the speech he was giving with animated gestures. He ignored his phone as it vibrated once in his pocket.

"As I'm sure you are all well aware," Jeremy said, speaking with his father's confident voice, "the acquisition of Brüding Pharmaceuticals represents a significant opportunity to increase SymbioTech's share of the biomedical consumer market. In the first year, we will recoup the total investment cost of the acquisition."

Heads nodded approvingly around the table. The only exception was a beak-nosed man named Lester Crowe. His face darkened when he met Jeremy's eyes, and his mouth twisted in a sneer. "Those are rather bold claims, don't you think?" he challenged. His tenor voice carried a distinctly Scottish accent, and his general temperament was one of conflict and complaint. Jeremy had been expecting his contestation since the start of the meeting.

"A bold claim, yes, but not without merit," Jeremy said. "Within the last five years, Brüding Pharma has grown in leaps and bounds. Their research and development department outpaces its closest competitors, and they will pose a significant threat to our economic security unless we act now." He straightened his crimson tie and cleared his throat, commanding even Crowe's attention. "We have the capital to buy out their executive board, and I know at least two of the seven sitting members are already in our pocket. Turn two more, and we will have the controlling interest of pharmaceuticals in Odols for the next twenty years."

Jeremy held his mutual glare with Lester Crowe, who remained stone-faced even as the rest of the room filled with applause. He felt his phone begin to vibrate persistently with an incoming phone call. He raised one finger in apology to the assembled group of executives and excused himself from the room. Once in the hallway, he raised the phone to his ear and winced as his wife's plaintive request arrived, unprompted, to his inner ear.

"Anna, I can't come home right now. I'm in the middle of a very important meeting."

"I can't find Jeremy," she said. "It's getting dark and Ellie says he hasn't been home all day." Annabelle sounded as nervous as he had ever heard her.

As Nathaniel, Jeremy sighed and looked at his watch. "I can leave in fifteen minutes. The entire executive board is here, and we are about to break ground on a new—"

"You can come home right now," Annabelle argued, "and the board be damned. I don't care how important these men think they are, your family comes first."

Jeremy nodded wearily and checked his watch again. "Family first," he agreed. "Of course. I'll be home as soon as I can."

He replaced the phone in his pocket and made sure his tie was perfectly straight. He stepped back into the conference room to apologize, and a moment later he called for a close to the meeting. The gathered men and women stared at him with blank, confused looks, but he was already out the door before they could protest, phone in his hand.

"Put me through to Kai," he said, and after a second

continued, "Dr. Kai. My driver will be downstairs in three minutes; I expect you to be waiting for me there." A pause. "Excellent," he said. "And bring your kit."

Jarringly, the vivid, *mad* hallucination ended.

Jeremy was abruptly back in bed, staring up into his father's gray eyes. He recoiled from the touch of his father's hand. Less than a second had passed; the slight smile which had graced his father's face slid away to be replaced by a thin frown.

He felt violently ill, as if he had been reading while riding a rollercoaster that had just pulled out of a quadruple corkscrew. It was motion sickness on steroids. The conference room, his father's conversation with his mother, the—well, everything— had been so real. His father asking a question was all that kept him anchored in reality.

"Jeremy, what were you doing so far from home?" Nathaniel asked, his voice at once regaining its former edge.

"I was exploring the Tower," Jeremy choked out. He bit back the bile that threatened to rise in his throat. His head was pounding worse than ever in the aftermath of his…experience, hallucination, whatever it was he had just gone through.

"You were exploring the tower," his father repeated. He rose and moved to stand by the fireplace once more. Jeremy glimpsed his father in the mirror, and he looked like he was wreathed in flames.

"Your mother was nearly hysterical when she came home to an empty house," he said quietly.

"I didn't mean to worry her—"

"And more than anything you disappointed me, Jeremy." His father turned, his gray eyes briefly ablaze before cooling, and he contemplated the wounded boy whose head was half-wrapped in fresh bandages. It covered both ears, wound beneath his chin, and was stained crimson by one of his temples.

"*I* was worried for you, Jeremy," he said, approaching the bed. Jeremy flinched back, afraid of making contact again, and his father stopped just outside of arm's reach. He crossed his arms as he addressed his son. "I don't know what I would have done if you had—" His father paused. He wasn't welling up with tears, on the verge of an emotional break; that would have been truly unnerving. He was simply taking a moment to choose his words.

"This," Nathaniel finally said, gesturing to Jeremy's bandaged head, "could have been so much worse."

Jeremy wasn't sure what to say. He hadn't been expecting a tearful confession or anything, but his father's words still spoke volumes. It was as close to a bonding experience as they'd had in years. He looked his father directly in the eyes.

"Family comes first," Jeremy said, his tone even.

Nathaniel eyed him appraisingly and nodded. He patted Jeremy's knee through the blankets and left the room without another word.

Unable to move, uncomfortably warm now beneath the blankets and basking in the fire's glow, Jeremy watched his father's shadow disappear down the hall. He didn't know what to make of the memories that lingered in his head, as fresh as if he had experienced them himself. His father had received the call about Jeremy's absence, he realized, just as he himself must have been lying unconscious on the floor of the Tower, head bleeding profusely against the cold stone.

And it had indeed been his father who rescued him from the old fort. That vision had flooded into him along with the others, as vivid as his own memories. Unbidden, the captured images overwhelmed his mind as he laid back down to rest.

His father had entered the first level of the Tower sometime after sundown, though light still filtered in through the windows of the second floor. His face had turned ashen when he saw Jeremy's motionless body lying against the stone table, and he'd carried him in both arms like a child. Nathaniel had stepped through the doorway of the ranch house while the moon hung low in the sky, and the next few hours had been frantic with Annabelle's fussing, Ellie's plaintive cries, and the attentive care of the doctor.

Another memory pushed to the fore, picking up earlier in the evening when his father had been leaving from work.

Jeremy emerged from the elevator and turned to see Dr. Kai waiting as he strode into the parking deck.

"Why am I here, sir?" she asked, her tone just barely on the side of tolerant politeness.

"I need some bloodwork drawn up discreetly, and I know you are loyal to this company and to me. I understand you requested updated equipment in the diagnostics lab."

Dr. Kai nodded.

"Consider it done," Jeremy said in his father's voice.

"Th-thank you, sir."

"Of course. And remember, absolute discretion."

The memory dissolved as a powerful wave of agony pulsed from Jeremy's temple and he lost his fight for consciousness.

CHAPTER NINE

BRENNAN ARRIVED JUST two minutes late of his estimate.

The apartment smelled stale, stagnant, and the specter of death loomed close by. He let himself in and marched straight back to his sister's room. A pair of lit candles feebly fought against the cloying odors emanating from Madison Warner's body, but they were no match for the final stages of her Fractured decay.

He was dismayed at the state in which he found her. It was obvious that she had not been able to leave her bed for several days. Her skin, once full and beautiful, now clung tightly against her bones, giving her face a hauntingly gaunt impression. The full bags under her eyes were colored like watery tea, and her eyes themselves were equally moist and ruddy. They stared lazily at one corner of the room, and she was either uncaring of Brennan's presence or unaware of it altogether. Her body writhed in bed, unattended, with her arms and legs shooting out violently at random intervals as she babbled at invisible phantoms.

Brennan grasped one of her clammy hands and held it between his own. He rubbed the top of it reassuringly as he spoke to her soothingly. "Maddy," he said. "Mads, I'm here. It's Arty."

His nephew, Greg Warner, appeared in the doorway. Greg was on the cusp of manhood, average height now but with a few inches still to grow. He brushed some of the dark hair from his eyes as he looked down on his ailing mother. "Thank you, Uncle Arty," he said, biting at his thumb. "She was like this when I got back. I did exactly what you told me to do, but I don't know, I guess it didn't work."

"When you got back?" Brennan echoed. "Why weren't you here? You're supposed to look after her!"

Greg's uncertain frown turned into a scowl. "I have a life, too, you know. It was only for an hour!"

"I send money to support you two," Brennan said, failing to keep the frustration out of his voice. "What was so important that—?"

His voice had risen to a near shout, and Maddy stirred beneath him in another bout of fitful struggling. Brennan gave his nephew a withering look and focused again on his ill sister. He held her down until the shaking ceased again. Her long-term patch use had left her body devastated. Brennan lifted the sleeves of her shirt to reveal her thin, pale arms. Faded scars lined both arms, their square shapes barely visible after years without using.

"She didn't get her hands on anything?" he asked, repeating the visual exam with her legs. Maddy moaned incoherently and pushed at his arms. Her eyes focused on the empty space behind him and followed something that could not be seen. Brennan frowned down at his older sister.

Greg shook his head. "She's getting worse, isn't she?"

The question twisted a knife in Brennan's heart. He knew that his sister might never recover from the damage her addiction had inflicted. It had robbed her of her family, her sanity, and now perhaps even her life. It was made worse by the fact that the moment the question was asked, in Brennan's heart of hearts he knew it to be true. Knowing the true nature of things was something he'd always been gifted with, though it felt like a curse in that moment.

"Right now, I think it's too soon to tell." He heard the falseness of his own words, but Brennan wanted to at least give his nephew the hope that they both longed for. "We'll do everything we can for her." That much was true.

"Of course," Greg said, nodding.

Maddy was back under control, and Brennan succeeded in getting her to drink some water. When he was sure she wouldn't relapse into spasms, at least not for the moment, he gestured to Greg to leave the room so they could let her rest. They retreated to the living room, where Brennan sat down directly across from his nephew.

He was tired. The case of Zachariah Nettle's murder wasn't any closer to being solved, and he realized that Bishop should have called him by now, or even earlier in the evening. He was about to enter a fourth day without sleep. And he was fairly certain that his nephew was lying to him, or at least not telling the whole truth.

His power had never led him wrong before, and of all the problems he could think of, this one was the most immediately reconcilable.

"Greg," he started, and he heard the detached detective tone of his own voice. "Do you love your mother?"

"Yes."

True.

"Would you do anything for her?"

"Of course."

True.

Brennan sighed deeply. "Why did you leave her

this afternoon?"

There was a fraction of a second when Greg hesitated before answering, but Brennan saw it. "I went to a friend's house," Greg said. "Just for an hour."

True.

"What did you do at your friend's place?"

"You know, just played games."

False.

"You're lying to me," Brennan growled.

"I swear I'm not!"

Brennan leaned forward and gripped the armrests of Greg's chair, his face only inches from his nephew's. Greg stared with wide eyes as Brennan searched his face. "Are you using, Greg?"

"What do you mean, using?"

"Don't play games with me!" His hold on the chair was painful, white-knuckled, but he was in control of his anger. Greg sunk back slightly into the cushion. "Patches. Are you using patches?"

"N-no, Uncle Arty," he stammered.

He didn't need his power's input to know that the kid was lying. Brennan sighed, grabbed his nephew by the arm, and tore his shirt's sleeve off at the shoulder. Greg shouted in protest, but Brennan's attention was entirely devoted to the blistering square of seared flesh, the signature mark of a patch. The drug was soaked up through the skin, and the strong toxins in the patch ate away at the flesh.

"You're lying," he growled, his hand tightly gripping Greg by the elbow.

Greg tried unsuccessfully to squirm out of his grasp. "Okay, I did it once. Today was the first time."

False.

Brennan gave his nephew a look which barred any contention, and Greg's face crumpled. Words started spilling out of his mouth, tripping over one another to get out in the open.

"Almost two years now," he admitted. He sounded guilty—ashamed, even—though no color rose in his cheeks. "But it's fine. I never use too many at once, and it isn't often. I have it under control."

"Your mother never thought she was abusing the patches either."

Greg scowled. "You have no idea what it has been like living here. With her. She can go days without recognizing me. When she does talk to me, it isn't really me she is seeing, but as if she's talking to somebody she wants me to be. Her ideal son. Or maybe an old friend of hers, I don't know. The way she is now is the way she has been for years." He made a crazy sign with one hand. "Completely detached."

"Watch it," Brennan growled. "She's still your mother. And my big sister."

Greg held up his hands. "I'm sorry, but it's true."

Brennan could feel that truth, which stung worse than the words themselves. He had no idea that his sister's condition had deteriorated to such a level. Or maybe he had simply not wanted to see it.

"So one night," Greg continued, "I was curious. I took one of the patches from her nightstand when she was in one of her stupors. It was incredible." His voice became mystified as he recalled the memory. "The room started swirling, like when you get the spins from drinking too much—"

Brennan gave him an even look.

"—which I would have absolutely no idea about."

He gave a skeptical harrumph.

Greg's eyes glazed over. "And when you're patched, it's like—you're free of everything. You see the world not for what it is but what it should be. The perfect world. You're a free spirit." The mystified tone left his voice. "Then that world breaks apart, and you'll do anything to get back to it."

Brennan lightly shook Greg's horribly burned arm. "This is the price for that 'perfect world'," he said dryly before releasing his grip. He stood up and backed away from his nephew.

If what his nephew said was true—and he knew that it was—then the patch had made a fantasy world for Maddy to escape to, even as it caused her real life to crumble around her. She was in that world even now.

"You're not mad at me, are you?" Greg asked.

"Mad?" Brennan supposed he should have been, seeing as how he was the only real adult in the kid's life, a life which was on the verge of being hopelessly wasted. "I'm not mad. Disappointed, I should say. You're a bright kid, Greg, when you aren't repeating your mother's mistakes." It hurt to speak ill of his sister, but he had to be honest with himself; she had made some terrible choices, and her son was now flirting with following that same path.

Greg, for his part, mostly just stared down into his lap. He chewed his lip and went to bite his fingernails several times, always checking the motion before his hand reached his mouth. Brennan realized that he was probably itching for a patch, even now.

"I'm taking all of the patches you have here," Brennan said. "Now."

"What?" Greg looked up in alarm. "Why?"

"Really? You're really asking me that?"

Greg stood, and though he was a full head shorter and a hundred pounds lighter, he stared directly into Brennan's eyes. "I don't have anything here," he said.

False.

Greg's eyes wavered, unable to keep focused on one spot for long, and they darted to one side as he licked his lips. Brennan raised an eyebrow and started walking in the direction of his nephew's nervous gaze. "There's nothing here," Greg repeated, a hint of desperation in his voice.

The apartment was small, and space was at a premium. Chairs and tables were arranged in just the right way to allow for legs to pass by, yet Brennan noticed a wide-backed chair positioned strangely against one wall. Sitting in it would have been awkward for conversations, and it didn't directly face the television, either. Ignoring his nephew's plaintive noises, Brennan grabbed the back and one arm of the chair and shoved it aside. Behind it, set low in the wall, was a black metal ventilation grate no larger than his hand.

"See? Nothing," Greg declared quickly. "What are you—?"

Brennan silenced him with a raised hand and knelt down to peer into the vent. It was dark, but he could just barely make out the shimmer of plastic about a foot inside. His fingers looped around the fine metal filigree and pulled, and the vent pried free of its casing. He reached in with one hand, cringing as he broke a fresh spider's web, and tightened his hand around the small bag inside. It was full of two-inch square patches.

"You can't just come in here and take my stuff!"

"I'm a cop, Greg. You're lucky I'm not arresting you right now. That's what would be happening if it were anyone but me."

"This is an illegal search and seizure," Greg argued. He made a grab for the bag of patches, but Brennan held him back with a stiff arm.

"No, this is a concerned family member holding a cold-turkey intervention." He marched into the kitchen and tossed the patches into the trash bin, then lifted the trash bag out and pulled the elastic bands tight. "Is this everything?"

Greg nodded sullenly.

"Say it out loud."

"Yes," he said through gritted teeth.

True.

"Good." Brennan felt the tension easing out of his face, and he placed a fatherly hand on Greg's shoulder as he looked his nephew in the eye. "I'm serious about this. You cannot go near this stuff. It's toxic, and I can't let you follow your mother's path."

"I'm not having nearly as much—"

"Greg! This is not a negotiation. What your mother is going through…" His voice trailed off as he shook his head. "I should have been looking out for her. It's my fault that she is the way she is now. I won't make that mistake again."

His heart chilled slightly at his own revelation. He had never admitted, never recognized before, that his sister might not have been Fractured if only he'd been more attentive. Even if it was just a speech to set his nephew on the right path, there was a vein of truth to it as well.

"There's something else you should know," Greg said quietly.

"What is it?"

"I told you how it feels to be patched, right? How liberating it is? Well, it also makes me see things…"

"It's a hallucinogen, Greg. Whatever you saw was just an illusion."

Greg bit the corner of his lip and frowned. "That's just it, though. It felt so real, and it concerned your partner, the lady cop."

"Bishop?" His eyebrows stitched together in confusion. "Why would you be hallucinating about her?"

"I'm trying to tell you, I think it was more than just the drug!" Greg ran a nervous hand through his hair. "She was lying there on the stage, surrounded in blood. Her clothes were drenched with it, and she was holding her hands against her stomach like she had been shot."

Brennan wasn't sure what to believe. It sounded like a horrible trip, except his power was telling him that Greg's story was true. "You think you had some sort of…what? A vision?"

Greg shrugged. "Maybe. There are always

psychics claiming to know the future, right?"

"They're always charlatans, though," Brennan said, perfectly aware of his own hypocrisy. Here he was, a human lie-detector, denouncing the possibility of psychics. "Bishop is fine. There's nothing to worry about."

Greg nodded slowly. "Yeah, you're probably right," he said. He didn't sound entirely convinced. There was a long, silent pause.

"You mentioned a stage?"

"It looked like some kind of theatre," Greg said, with another one of his patented shrugs.

"We're in luck, then," Brennan said, suddenly grinning. "Bishop hates the theatre."

A reluctant smile formed on Greg's lips. "How fortunate. Still, if you two do see a play or something, maybe you should go in first."

"That doesn't sound very gentlemanly of me."

"Is that a word? And chivalry is nice and all, but it might get her killed."

Brennan looked at his nephew for a moment before forcing a smile. He hefted the trash bag over his shoulder as he turned to leave. "Get some sleep," he said. "And take care of yourself!"

"You should sleep, too, Uncle Arty. You look like death."

"Hey, death wished—ah, forget it."

φ φ φ

BRENNAN AWOKE THE next morning to a message in his voicemail.

"Arthur, it's Noel. Sorry for the late call, I figured you'd be awake. Guess you needed the sleep, though. God knows we both do." There was a small laugh. "Anyway, I visited the pharmacy where Nettle worked. Turns out he had had a casual girlfriend, but she'd only come by once or twice, and not a word of her in the past few months. I asked around, but nobody knew any more than that. Sounds like they were over a while ago, which leaves us back at square one. I'm going to grab some zees before I go mad. See you at the station."

Brennan hadn't meant to fall asleep in the first place, and he rubbed the crustiness from his eyes. In the bathroom, he wiped a wetted hand across his face and stared at himself in the mirror. The sleep had been dreamless, and he felt as if he had gotten no rest at all. The clock indicated it was a quarter to eight. He thought about what Bishop had said in her message.

No ex-girlfriend, at least not recent enough to make a real suspect of her. It wasn't much, but it narrowed down the direction of the investigation. If it wasn't a domestic dispute gone wrong, then there was something much more sinister afoot. But there were too many inconsistencies to make heads or tails of what happened that night.

Brennan shaved, changed clothes, and walked across the street to the station. Odols Police Department was housed in a squat, ugly building that was dwarfed by the high-rise apartment complexes and business offices that rose up on all sides. This late in the morning, nearly everybody was already at work. Bishop looked better rested than she had in days. The change a few hours of sleep could make was a minor miracle.

"What happened to you? Did you sleep on the curb?"

"Good morning to you, too, sweetheart," Brennan said to her, affecting his best impersonation of Sam.

Bishop shuddered. "Don't you start on that. If you ever asked me on a date, it would be too weird."

"You aren't my type."

"Strong-willed? Independent? Blonde?"

"Short."

"Go to Hell."

"Not yet! I'm not quite ready to die." He poured himself a steaming cup of what passed as coffee and joined Bishop at her desk. She had the Zachariah Nettle files already spread out.

"I'm assuming you got my voicemail," she said,

and he grunted the affirmative. "I've been looking at these files all morning and there is one thing I'm confused about."

Brennan raised an eyebrow. "One thing? I looked at these all day yesterday and turned up nothing. In fact, since you ruled out the girlfriend angle, I think we've actually lost ground. Nothing seems to add up."

Bishop smiled ruefully. "That's what I thought at first, too. Inconsistencies abound with Zachariah. He should have been poor by all rights, just scraping by on his pharmacist's salary, but the things he had in his apartment said otherwise."

"Actually, I looked into that," Brennan said. "Pharmacists pull in a lot more than we thought. Six-figure salaries, and that's just within a few years out of college."

"Really? Maybe I should change careers," Bishop mused aloud. "But still, without financial help from his parents? He should have had student loans to pay off. That kind of education wouldn't have come cheap."

"He was living pretty luxuriously, from what I saw."

"Exactly. And as far as we can tell, nothing was stolen, so burglary isn't a likely motive. I think whoever came to visit Zachariah already had murder in their heart, and I'm relatively certain it has something to do with the extra money."

Brennan scratched at his chin; he had missed some stubble. "If that's true, then we're looking at some pretty serious suspects. Mobsters, gangsters, junkies and their dealers, loan sharks—the list goes on. Anybody who had money to give and the means to take it back when the time came. We could search half the city and not find our guy."

"True," she allowed, "but the suspect pool gets a lot shallower once you look closer at the victim's body."

"Did our guy leave behind fingerprints? Or some stray hair?"

Bishop sighed. "Unfortunately, nothing so obvious. But we can be reasonably certain that Zachariah knew his killer, and that the attack was induced by some horrible fit of rage. When we saw that Nettle's eyes had been removed, I thought it had to have been someone who was ashamed to be seen by the victim as a murderer. That profile pointed toward a family member or intimate lover."

"Both of which we eliminated," Brennan pointed out.

"Right. But once those options were gone, it left the question of why the killer took the eyes. And then it suddenly dawned on me!" She swiveled in her chair and brought up the computer screen. She spoke while she typed. "I asked the lab techs to analyze a tissue sample of the skin around his eyes, where we saw…ah, here it is. Remember the skin irritation we saw at the crime scene? It was caused by some kind of corrosive substance, not a result of the knife gouging the eyes out."

Brennan followed her train of thought. "So we don't have a motive yet, but you think the killer removed Nettle's eyes because he was covering his tracks?"

She nodded. "Whatever the substance was, our killer thinks it can be traced back to him."

"Was the lab able to determine what exactly we're dealing with?"

"Unfortunately, no. There wasn't enough tissue to work with. But considering Nettle's profession, I'm thinking it's something you might find in a pharmacy."

"Something you'd find in a pharmacy," Brennan echoed. "So if there's something missing from Zachariah's workplace—"

"Then we can find out what burned our victim's eyes—"

"And follow the clues back to our murderer!" Brennan finished triumphantly. His grin was mirrored on Bishop's lips, and they stared at each other in mutual excitement.

"Well, aren't you two just adorable?"

Brennan was surprised by the familiar voice. He

looked up to see Sam leaning casually against the glass divider with the hallway. Sam was watching them with an amused look sprawled across his face.

"Sam," he said. "What are you doing here? Don't get me wrong, it's always a pleasure, but…"

"But you didn't call me, I know," Sam finished. He gestured to Bishop. "I'm actually here to pick up that one."

"Noel?" Brennan's eyebrows reached for the ceiling as he turned to her. "You asked him to come here?"

Bright crimson flowed high into her cheeks, though it was impossible to tell whether from anger or embarrassment. "We are working together on the case, so yes, I asked him to come as a consultant. Only to consult on the case," she stressed, looking Sam pointedly in the eye. He nodded, his solemn expression belied by his amused, dancing eyes.

The light perfume, revitalized energy, and visibly happier demeanor all suddenly made sense. Brennan glanced incredulously between the two of them.

"You two are going on a date?"

Sam held up his hands. "Hey, I'm just a paid consultant. I wouldn't know a date if it called me up out of the blue and asked me to brunch. Certainly not after impromptu drinks together the night before."

The blush in Bishop's cheeks deepened.

Brennan shook his head. "This is a dream. A crazy, delusional dream and the Sleepers are coming for me soon."

"It isn't a date," Bishop said firmly. "And I needed a strong drink after the day I had yesterday. Sam happened to be there, and he offered to pay. Then I walked home, alone. Which is exactly what will happen today," she finished, directing the last part at Sam.

True, chimed the little voice in Brennan's head.

As he watched them go, his right hand fell unconsciously over his left, where his fingers touched upon the smooth metal of his commitment to Mara. His heart still ached for her after so many years. He waited until Sam and Bishop were out of sight before collecting his things and heading back home.

CHAPTER TEN

JEREMY HAD NEVER let go of a dream so reluctantly.

He had been reliving a memory, one very familiar to him.

In the Jardin des Anges he stood, admiring the beautiful flowers as an equally lovely specimen of a woman, her arm looped in his, leaned gently into him and rested her head against his shoulder. A harpist played soothing music from an obscure corner of the gardens, the notes dancing softly in the air as they were carried by the wind.

"Annabelle," he said.

The blonde, blue-eyed girl stirred from her reverie and looked up at him with the most heart-warming smile. "Yes, my love?"

"I think this is the best date we've ever been on."

"Really?" she asked, her smile deepening. "You aren't bored to tears yet? I was sure that a visit to the Jardin des Anges

would finally scare you away."

"I never said I wasn't bored," he grinned, pulling her in for a kiss that lasted several seconds. "But I love you." Her eyes glittered in response to that. "I love you, and you will have to try so much harder to dissuade me."

"Mmm. Maybe I don't feel like trying all that hard," she cooed, melting into his embrace.

"Good." He kissed the top of her head.

They started walking toward the exit of the Jardin.

"I'm just glad you didn't get down on one knee," Annabelle said. "If I get proposed to someday, I want it to be an intimate moment, not surrounded by strangers."

Jeremy had his free hand stuck deep in his pocket. He toyed with the small, velvety box that hid there, secreted away until the perfect moment. He feared that moment had just passed.

"A proposal? In the Garden? I wouldn't dream of it."

With a jarring transition, Jeremy awoke into the present. He was delirious for several moments as he took stock of the room. The fire had died down to smoldering embers, and the warmth of the room had greatly diminished with it. His head pounded and he was reluctant to leave the embrace of his bedcovers. He probably would have succumbed to the allure of further sleep if he hadn't smelled breakfast cooking.

Outside, the day was already well underway. Flowers of red and orange and blue opened up happily to the sun, greedily drinking in its energy. Even further, the orchards were in full bloom with pears and apples. *But not peaches*, Jeremy reminded himself. And even further out beyond those, almost invisible from the window, he could just make out the broad, rounded tops of the black walnut grove. A murder of crows flew in that direction.

The hardwood floor was cool on his bare feet and Jeremy hurried to slip on a pair of loafers. His bandages, he noticed by way of the mirror, had been changed. There was only a small, bright dot of red right over the source of the throbbing pain he felt. He was having difficulty wrestling with his father's memories; they felt so *real*, as real as any memory properly his own.

"Get your breakfast while it's hot or all of this will be for naught!" his mother called out loudly. Jeremy groaned inwardly at her rhyme as he padded his way quietly down the hallway to the kitchen.

To call the Scott country home a ranch was something of an understatement. Strong, wooden beams, as thick and rough as freshly felled trees, framed the residence over an area about the size of an acre. Floor-to-ceiling windows lined the south walls, and the golden sunlight filled the main lounging room. Shelves had been built into the chairs and couch, each one filled with books of all sizes and colors. Hardwood flooring was covered here and there by soft area rugs, upon which sat the furniture.

Adjacent to the lounging area was the kitchen; all polished stone and smooth granite, the kitchen was very modern with an aesthetic feel that somehow meshed with the natural décor of the rest of the house. In the kitchen was his mother, with an apron around her waist and her blonde hair pulled back into a bun.

"Hi, honey," she said, smiling sweetly at him as he entered. "I'm glad you're finally awake, it's been so quiet all morning."

"Morning, Ann—uh, Mom," he replied, covering his slip-up with a yawn. "I slept like the dead."

She looked at him worriedly for a moment.

"Breakfast," Jeremy said quickly, gesturing. "Smells good. Pancakes?"

"Of course, my baby's favorite."

"Mom," he groaned. He was hardly a baby anymore.

"Pancakes are just about finished, and I have scrambled eggs coming up in a few minutes. There's bread waiting to be toasted, butter and jam on the table. I'm guessing you want milk?"

"Yes, please," he said.

"Well you know where to find it," Annabelle replied, gesturing toward the fridge. He grinned to himself. She hadn't changed a bit in the twenty-three years he'd known her.

Jeremy frowned.

She was his mother. She was also Annabelle. His head throbbed as he struggled to make those two facts, the two sets of memories he held, compatible with one another.

His mother saw the stages of Jeremy's confusion play across his face but said nothing.

Another thready pulse of pain, only a minor irritation, and Jeremy shelved the problem. He poured himself a glass of milk from the carafe in the fridge and sat down at the table. In addition to the food his mother had listed, there was also sliced ham on a large plate, each sliver the size of Jeremy's hand.

"Wow, Mom, you made *way* too much food for just the four of us."

"The two of us, actually." His mother glanced at the door with a look of irritation. "Your father watched over you while you slept, but he was on his way right back to the city at the first light of day. He promised that it would only be for the morning, to finish the business meeting that was interrupted yesterday. He'll be back by this afternoon," she said, wearing her best smile for him.

If memory served him, he knew now that the cheer was false. Jeremy wasn't fooled. But he could still beg ignorance, for his mother's sake. He smiled in return as he sliced his stack of pancakes into quarters.

"You said the two of us. What about Ellie?" he asked.

His mother shook her head. "Wild child, that one. I've been trying to get her inside, but she'd rather get her hands and knees dirty chasing after rabbits."

Jeremy shrugged. "Her loss, more for me," he said, spearing a healthy portion of ham with his fork and depositing it on his plate. He ate like a ravenous wolf. He had never consumed as much in his life as he did that morning. The stack of pancakes, buttered and drowned in syrup, hardly made a dent in his appetite. The slices of ham, a half dozen total and each slice as thick as his pinky finger, brought his hunger down to a level approaching "gnawing". He followed the first tall glass of milk with an equal amount of orange juice. His thirst slaked, he scooped up the scrambled eggs with his pieces of toast and put them down with bites of prodigious size.

His mother smiled and filled her plate with a quarter as much food. "Easy, Jay, don't forget to chew." She regarded him a moment. "Or breathe."

Jeremy attempted to respond, stuffing food into his cheeks to make room for his mouth to work. It was completely unintelligible.

"Mum," he finally managed. It came out British-sounding by accident, by virtue of the food still in his mouth. "How did you manage to make—well, *everything*—taste so good?"

"Why, thank you, sweetheart. But it helps when the person eating it has been knocked on the head first." Her eyebrows furrowed with concern. "Are you sure you're feeling all right?"

"I'm feeling much better now," he said, smiling. He looked outside for a moment; Ellie ran past the window, giggling, followed closely by a small, red-furred squirrel. Jeremy's eyes returned to meet his mother's. "Mom, I'm curious how you and Dad met."

"Really?" she asked. "Surely we've mentioned it to you before, when you were younger. You probably just forgot."

He frowned and reflected, searching his memories. His father's recollections threatened to crowd out his own, though, and he struggled to find an original memory of his that told of his parents' first meeting.

"It's okay if you forgot," his mother interjected, "I don't mind talking about it." A small smile fluttered on her lips. "Your father was a very charismatic man when he was younger. Very charming. The two of us went to university together, as you know, though he was two years ahead of me." She pursed her lips in concentration. "It was the end of November, I remember. All of us were preparing for our end-of-term exams. And your father, well, he was in his senior year and already had a job lined up after graduation. It didn't matter what grades he received in the end, so long as he passed and got his diploma."

Here she paused, spreading her hands in front of her, a cautionary gesture. "You'll have to take his word for it, because he only told me this story after we were already dating for several months, but he *swears* that the first time he saw me his whole life changed. Heart skipped a beat, jaw dropped to the floor, tripped up head over heels; he was such a romantic back then, your father.

"Anyway, *I* am sure that I looked like a train wreck. My hair was a mess, I wasn't wearing any makeup; I had been practically living in the library for the last several days. And in walks your father, tall and handsome, with a nice smile and kind eyes, and the moment I saw him, I knew."

She leaned in conspiratorially. "I knew he would be the death of me. He was all grace and collectedness and I was a mess, flustered over finals and papers for which I was in no way prepared. His eyes met mine and he walked directly toward me, never breaking stride from entering the room, and stopped just a half-step away from where I was seated. He said—and I'll never forget this—he said, 'When did angels stop living in the Jardin des Anges and start studying in the library?'"

Jeremy choked on his last piece of toast, snorting

with sudden laughter. "He said that?" he asked incredulously. His mother laughed as well.

"Your father has always had a way with words. He knows *exactly* what to say, as well as how and when to say it. If he had been any less serious, I would have blown him off, and if he had tried an actual, suave pickup line, I would have screamed at him in frustration to let me study in peace." She chuckled to herself. "As it was, I was speechless. It was my jaw's turn to drop, and I just stared at him with wide eyes. He had spoken loud enough for the entire room to hear, which only made it more surreal."

"So what happened next?" Jeremy asked.

Ellie burst into the house, slamming open the screen door with youthful exuberance as she cried "Mommy, Mommy, Mommy!" and threw herself into her mother's embrace. Only too late did Annabelle realize that her daughter was liberally covered in grass, leaves and mud. Lots of mud. Jeremy grinned to himself. Perhaps he had given too much credit to his sister's maturity.

"Ellie!" she cried out. Her white apron was already soaking up the moist mud. She sighed. "Jeremy, do you mind? I've got to make sure this one is cleaned up, *right now*." She emphasized the last words at Ellie, who squealed in delight as she was tickled under her arms. "I'll tell you the rest of the story later?" she suggested.

Jeremy made a split-second decision and steeled himself against the nausea he knew was coming. "Sure thing, Mom," he said, touching her lightly on her exposed arm. A rush of memories flooded over him, disorienting in speed and vividness, and he was thankful that he was already sitting down.

Before his mother had even stood from the table, Jeremy already knew everything.

CHAPTER ELEVEN

DETECTIVE BRENNAN WOKE in a hospital.

He was sitting in an uncomfortable leather chair with metal armrests, and his neck twinged from sleeping at an awkward angle. There was very little to be heard going on in the hallway, and a glance at the clock confirmed that it was very early in the morning, hours before dawn. A steady series of beeps toned from a machine. The room was otherwise quiet.

He turned and looked at the pale woman lying prostrate in bed. She had a slender face, gentle lips and early laugh lines around the eyes. Had she been awake, Brennan knew, blue eyes like sapphires would have glimmered back at him. When the two of them had met, she had been a rare kind of beauty. Beyond her pleasant looks, she had borne a steady strength within her. She had a compassionate heart and loved those around her more than seemed possible, and wherever she would go, smiles would appear.

His wife, Mara. She had been the greatest gift to this world, the single saving grace of Arthur's life. That had been before she Fractured.

Now, the skin clung tightly to her bones, making her fine cheeks stark, almost mountainous protrusions on a light, deeply sloping landscape. Her eyes sunk deep in their sockets, dark as bruises against her ghostly complexion. Her hair grew out long and thin, untended to, sickly. Her gentle lips, so pink and luscious before, were now an ugly purple.

A knock on the door, and a man in a long, white coat entered quietly.

"Mr. Brennan," he said, "can I speak with you for a moment? Out here, in the hallway, please."

Arthur rose heavily from the chair and followed the doctor out of the room. He had not recognized the chill before, but he realized that the hallway was considerably warmer than Mara's room. The nurses' station was empty except for one, and she was dozing at her desk. The hallway was otherwise deserted.

"Mr. Brennan," the doctor began solemnly, "I cannot tell you how sorry I am. You have my condolences."

Brennan leveled a look at the shorter man. "My Mara isn't dead."

The doctor nodded sympathetically. "I understand that this is a difficult time for you, but there is nothing more we can do for your wife. She can be kept on life support for a time, but I would not be optimistic for a change in her condition. We can move her to Ridgewood, a long-term care facility, but—"

Brennan shook his head. "She would want me to keep fighting for her. Her body is still here, and I know her mind is in there, somewhere." Now the doctor shook his head slowly, unconsciously. They were effectively alone, but his voice dropped to a whisper. "A Sleeper could go in, find her, bring her back—"

"Sleepers are myths, Mr. Brennan," the doctor said. His eyes screamed concern for Brennan's mental well-being. "And even if they weren't, it's a fool's errand to go tampering with a Fractured brain. The best thing to do is to let her go peacefully."

Brennan held back his emotions. They raged against his heart and soul like rapids against a dam; one slip of his control would open the floodgates. He willed away the tears for his lost wife. She wasn't lost, he reminded himself. He would not allow it.

"Then I will go myself," he said softly.

"Then you're a…" The doctor gazed wide-eyed, mouth agape. "That…would be madness." He shook his head, and his voice regained some vestige of strength. "Even if you could, I would not allow it. It would be suicide."

Brennan felt numb inside. He knew that what the doctor said was the truth. But while his mind could understand, his heart still rebelled. His thoughts had turned sluggish even as his heart raced. How dare this man presume to know what was best for his wife, what was best for him. But that was it, wasn't it? He was no longer thinking of Mara, but rather only of himself. He was the one who wasn't ready for her to go.

Something in the air changed. Maybe it was a pressure shift from an opened door, or perhaps his ears heard something his brain didn't register, but Brennan was abruptly aware of another presence.

There, over the doctor's shoulder, he saw a man who had not been there the previous moment. He was slender of build and wore a nurse's outfit, scrubs of light blue. There was an intensity in his stare that was unnerving.

For a moment, the entire scene held in perfect stillness. The doctor's mouth hung in mid-air, an unspoken word frozen on his lips. The *beep beep beep* from Mara's room had gone silent. The newcomer nurse, however, moved with a gentle grace that Brennan was familiar with, once upon a time. Moving with caution, as if any abrupt movements would shatter their reality, the male nurse reached for the back waistband of his scrubs and retrieved a small pistol.

Brennan struggled with his body. Instead of being frozen in place like the doctor, he moved with the alacrity of one wading through chest-deep pudding. A single step took an eternity. A heavy pressure fell upon his chest, stealing the wind from his lungs. He gasped for breath as he tightly closed his fist. Sharp pain shot through his palm, jerking his arm with unexpected speed. The slowing, painful pressure around him vanished.

Brennan leapt to the side as a bullet sped from the gun. He crashed through the door to Mara's room, the impact accompanied by the sound of breaking glass, not the thud of solid wood he'd expected. He glimpsed her prone form one last time before the entire world shattered around them.

φ φ φ

HE WOKE FROM the nightmare to find himself in his apartment. At some point in the afternoon, he had succumbed carelessly to sleep while reclining in the leather chair. From the chair, he had leapt upon the low, glass table in the center of the room and shattered it. Slivers of glass sliced scores of small cuts on his face and arms and made a mess of his shirt, but it was better than staying in the nightmare with the Sleeper for one moment longer.

He stood and brushed some of the glass from his body, taking care not to push any shards in deeper than they already were. Still cradled in one hand was a small, sharp thumbtack, and a slim trail of blood trickled from where it had punctured his palm. It would join the several dozen other such scars.

He stumbled to the kitchen and grabbed his phone from the counter before going into the bathroom. He dialed Sam's number and told him to meet him at the apartment in fifteen minutes. He caught his reflection in the mirror.

"Better make that twenty minutes."

"Can do, partner."

He placed the phone on the sink countertop and shed his clothes. He let the shower run for a few minutes, then winced as he stepped into the steaming-hot water. Red rivulets ran from a dozen minor cuts. He groaned as the warmth spread through his body, relieving tension he hadn't realized he'd been holding. The cuts stung, but the pain was manageable.

When he felt ready, he used tweezers to remove the slender pieces of glass that remained in his skin. It was ugly and painful, and at one point he accidentally stepped on one of the fallen shards and had to remove it once more from his foot, but he managed it. Brennan closed his eyes as he let the water flow over his face. After what had seemed to be only seconds, a polite knock came from the front door. It devolved into heavy poundings with a fist by the time Arthur had dried and dressed himself.

"Come on, some people are trying to sleep," he grumbled, opening the door for Sam.

"No, they aren't, it's three in the—Jesus, you look like hell."

"Is that an improvement from looking like death?"

"Certainly not." Sam eyed the living room as he entered. "Your furniture giving you trouble?"

"Yeah, table got out of line, acting like it owned the place. I showed it who pays the rent around here."

Sam nodded. "So, what's up?"

Brennan grabbed two Cokes from the fridge and passed one to Sam. "Bring me up to speed on the case. What did you and Bishop discuss over brunch?"

He huffed and sat on one of the bar stools. "Never got brunch. Her idea of a date was us going back to where Zachariah Nettle worked and getting a full look at their logbook. Everything in and out of the pharmacy over the past three months."

"It wasn't a date," Brennan corrected.

"Yeah, well, clearly. I guess she's having trouble admitting her feelings for me."

"You slept with another woman while you two were dating."

Sam shrugged. "Women. So territorial. It's not as if we had agreed to be exclusive—" He caught Brennan's look. "Right. Getting off topic. Noel flashed her badge and we got everything we asked for. Looked over the logs for about an hour—you wouldn't *believe* how much traffic a pharmacy gets, these were no quick reads—and we saw some interesting figures."

"What did you find?"

"Everything in the books was solid except for one product. NicoClean, some kind of prescription nicotine patch for chronic smokers who want to quit. These patches came in huge amounts each month, I'm talking *boxes* of the stuff, and sold out every two weeks like clockwork. Patches come in, patches go out."

"Patches..." Brennan murmured. It was familiar.

"Now, get this," Sam continued. "The pharmacy says they weren't even aware of so many boxes of NicoClean being sold, and the financials match. Their profits only match for a fraction of what the record says was sold. And I bet you can guess who was working each time a large quantity of NicoClean was sold."

"Zachariah Nettle."

"Exactamundo!"

"Are NicoClean patches worth that much on the street?"

McCarthy faltered. "Well, that's the thing...they

aren't. The mesh is a bit thicker, so it can hold more nicotine per patch, and it gets in the bloodstream faster than the generic stuff, but if you're looking for a quick fix then you'd just light up the old-fashioned way."

"And nobody would buy nicotine patches in dark alleys and on street corners."

"Exactamundo," Sam said, less enthusiastically. "We've got nothing."

"No," Brennan said. "This is too close to our victim, there has to be something here."

McCarthy leaned against the counter, a mocking smile on his lips. "You know, as much fun as it is reading pharmaceutical records and looking at your ugly mug, I don't do this work for free."

Brennan grunted. "Bishop hired you this time. Look to her for money."

Sam's eyes lit up. "Ah, I see. Go collect from the lady for, ah, services rendered." He winked. "Gotcha."

"I want you to explain that to her using those exact words. Then we'll see who has the ugly mug."

Sam shook his head and hooked a thumb over his shoulder. "So, you going to explain your grievance with the table?"

Brennan frowned. The motion hurt, and he turned away from Sam as he grimaced. "Not yet," he said. "Perhaps another time."

Sam gave him a long stare. "Another time, partner."

CHAPTER TWELVE

IT WAS WELL into the afternoon when Jeremy heard the front door open noisily.

The sun was settling in among the mountains, and it would soon disappear from view. For now, light filtered in through the windows of Jeremy's room, casting a golden hue on the whitewashed walls and solid wood beams. He was sitting up in bed, struggling with a book from his summer reading list, when a bass-like voice bellowed out a greeting from the kitchen.

"Hellooooo!" The absurdly loud roar could only belong to one man. "I brought presents and souvenirs, but I guess there aren't any kids here."

He was sixteen and hardly a kid anymore, but Jeremy leapt excitedly to his feet and raced to the kitchen. Ellie had already beaten him there, and she was scooped up by a pair of enormous hands, connected by beefy, hairy forearms to the largest man Jeremy had ever met. His naturally faded jeans were frayed around the ankles, and a spattering of mud stains clung to his pant legs. A weathered plaid shirt strained against his broad chest. A tuft of dark hair reached up through the neck of it, and he had an untrimmed beard of several months' growth. Ellie writhed in his grasp as he tickled her under her arms and around the waist, and she was breathless when he finally released her.

"Jay!" he boomed. His voice was deep and rumbled through the room like thunder through the sky.

"Uncle Rick!" Jeremy ran into his uncle's welcoming embrace.

The older man was rocked back on his heels. "Whoa there. When did my nephew get replaced by this giant? Last time I saw you, you were barely this high," he said, holding a hand by his waist. He smiled as Jeremy laughed and pulled away.

"We weren't expecting to see you," Jeremy said.

Ellie grinned and shook her head emphatically. "Where have you been? Where's Dad?"

"Carrying my little brother's bags," Nathaniel grunted as he crossed the threshold of the front door. He heaved a pair of heavy traveling backpacks through the doorway, one strap in each hand. "Because apparently I'm a pack mule. How in the world did you carry those things?"

Uncle Rick grinned and winked at Jeremy and Ellie. "It's a secret. Only international men of mystery such as myself can know."

"Fine," Nathaniel grumbled. "My international brother of mystery can carry them the rest of the way to the guest room."

"We can help!" Ellie volunteered, rushing over to one of the bags. Her reed-thin body bowed as she heaved at one of the straps, but the bag hardly moved. She settled down on the ground instead and started to unzip one of the larger pockets.

"Hold on there, little lady," Uncle Rick said, casually lifting the bag away with one hand. "No presents until after dinner. That's your mother's rule."

"And you'll tell us all about where you've been?" Jeremy asked.

Uncle Rick let out his rumbling laugh again. "But of course! There will be jungles with temples, hidden treasure from the bottom of the ocean, bizarre rituals from secluded tribes—"

"You brought us treasure?!" Ellie bounced up and down, her hair flapping madly with each jump.

Uncle Rick winked. "You will see. *After dinner.*" He slung a bag over each massive shoulder and walked away to the ranch's guest room.

"He's hiding something good in those bags," Ellie said greedily.

"After dinner," Jeremy parroted, and he left her alone in the kitchen as he returned to his room. It was still warm, and red coals smoldered silently in the fireplace. Jeremy felt a sensation of unease that had nothing to do with the heat of the room. He had not expected Uncle Rick's arrival, but these visits were always a surprise. His father was ordinarily frustrated by them, but he seemed perfectly aware of the arrangement today. Perhaps he had mentioned it in conversation and Jeremy had forgotten about it.

Jeremy reached up and gingerly touched his bandages. His head ached more strongly now, and the assigned reading would do little in the way of distracting him from his pain. He sighed, left the room again, and walked back to the kitchen. Ellie had disappeared, probably off playing with squirrels.

His mother entered as he was reaching for the medicine cabinet. She had a bushel of freshly picked pears from the orchard supported under one arm. "Jay, I saw the car out front. Where is your father?"

"He's helping Uncle Rick with his bags," Jeremy said off-hand, reaching for the bottle of painkillers.

His mother froze in place. She looked between the front door and the hall that led to the guest bedroom before settling back on Jeremy. Her face calmed, and her features smoothed over. The change had been less than a second long, but he had seen it all the same.

"Is there something wrong?" he asked.

"Not at all," she replied. "I just wasn't expecting your uncle, that's all."

Jeremy shrugged. He let the tap fill a glass with water, then threw back two of the white tablets. "My head has been bothering me," he explained, in response to his mother's inquisitive stare.

She nodded and placed the fruit basket on the counter. "All right, well let me know if it gets worse. We might need to take you to the hospital for a scan."

"I'm sure I'll be fine," Jeremy said, forcing as much cheer into his voice as he could. He wasn't sure what else they might find if they scanned his head. Whatever was going on with the memories freaked him out more than he cared to admit.

When his father's hand had brushed against his during his recovery, Jeremy had thought the world was ending. His head had erupted in searing pain, and the memory came unexpectedly—and it was so *vivid*. He thought back on it and it came as clearly in his head as his own memories of venturing to the Tower, playing with Ellie in the garden, and picking fruit with his mother in summers past. They were more than just a part of his father—they were now a part of *him*. And there was so much to go through.

He left his mother and returned to his room. The infernal book from his summer reading list was still open to the first page, which was as far as he had managed to concentrate with the pain in his head. The painkillers would need more time to take effect, so he went to move it away. As he lifted it from the bed, however, a sudden realization came over him. He had not even passed the first page, but he already knew what was going to happen in this chapter. And the second, and third, and so on, all the way to the end of the book. It was a fuzzy memory, but it was there. He flipped to the last page of the book and read it, just to be sure.

He had read this book before.

But it was impossible. The price tag was still on the back cover; they had bought the books on his and Ellie's summer reading lists at the beginning of summer, but this was the first time it had been opened. The crisp paper still crinkled as the spine flexed in his grip, and Jeremy understood where he had read it before.

It was his father's memory.

Somehow, more than just that first flash of memory had made the trip into his head. As he thought about it, concentrating, the pain in his head increased tenfold. And he remembered so much more.

None of them were *his* memories, but they belonged to him all the same. Places he had never visited, people he had never met, all flashed through his mind. A rush came over him.

He flipped open a notebook and took a pen in his left hand. He was a righty, but his father was left-handed. He wrote out his signature—*Nathaniel Scott*—on the page. It was an exact copy, except for when he thought about it a little too consciously and marred the double-T at the end of 'Scott'.

He looked down at the book again. *The Picture of Dorian Gray*—it had been years since he had read it. He opened it to the first page and read, "The studio was filled with the rich odour of roses, and when the light summer wind stirred amidst the trees of the garden, there came through the open door the heavy scent of the lilac, or the more delicate perfume of the pink-flowering thorn." The words greeted him like old friends—the passage was made familiar again. He looked around at the changed room in which he found himself.

The cheap linoleum was cold beneath his feet. A foldout table was propped against one wall, with three low stools sitting around it. He held a worn book in his hands, a secondhand copy with a sticker on the back indicating the library's ownership of it.

The room was small and dank. Mildew crept out from

beneath the peeling wallpaper. He studiously ignored the shouting and sounds of crashing glass from the apartment next door. Beyond the mildew was the smell of something else, like warm beer left in the sun for too long. It was late, and he read by the light of the streetlamp filtering in through the dirty window. He didn't know where his father was, but that was a good thing; better elsewhere than here. His brother was gone, too, which bothered him somewhat more.

"Derrick?" he asked. Empty silence answered him.

He got up and walked into the only other room in the cramped apartment. A queen-sized mattress and a bunk-bed dominated the room, and what little space remained was taken up by a dresser that held clothes for the three of them. The room was dark, and his eyes hadn't adjusted yet.

"Rick?" he called again, but his words were swallowed in the black.

It wasn't altogether surprising; Rick often strayed from home, especially when he knew their father wouldn't find out. He was a wanderer by nature. But it always made it worse for the few times he was missing when their father stumbled home.

Somebody was calling out a name now, but it wasn't his. The neighbors were still going at it.

He turned back and ducked into the tiny bathroom that he never considered a full room. The shower worked, but irregularly, and even then, it ran only cold water. Here, too, the wallpaper was folding in on itself. He washed his hands under the frigid tap in the sink and ran wet fingers through his untidy hair.

His eyes were bright and blue—though he could have sworn they had always been dark gray—and shadows crept in beneath the lids. A messy rag of blond hair sat atop his head. Despite having eaten little for as long as he could remember, his cheeks held a youthful fullness that was unfamiliar to him. There was a gash on his temple, too, from some wound he didn't remember. It oozed through the bandage he hadn't felt before.

Somebody was calling his name.

His name. He remembered all of a sudden that he was Jeremy. Jeremy Scott. Blue eyes, light-blond hair, bleeding head. *Bleeding head.* There was something important about that.

"Jay, hold still," he heard a woman saying. *Annabelle,* his memory supplied.

"Anna…"

"Jeremy, sweetie, it's going to be all right."

"What happened?" It was his brother—no—his *uncle,* Rick.

"I don't know. I was coming to get him for dinner and he was lying on the floor."

"How long was he like that?"

"I don't *know,*" Annabelle said, an edge to her voice. "Here, help me get him up."

Jeremy felt himself being lifted up by strong arms and cradled against a solid chest, and a moment later he was back in his bed with a *whumph.* They covered him with a heavy comforter that smothered him and he felt like he was in a furnace, but lying on his bed again was like resting on a cloud. He stopped trying to keep his eyes open; it was just too difficult. He fell unconscious.

Chapter Thirteen

THE SHUTTLE CARRIED Brennan around the city rim to the far side of Odols.

He disembarked a short distance from the pharmacy where Zachariah Nettle had worked. The store was a few blocks from Nettle's apartment, still part of the same rough neighborhood. Unsavory types leaned against rundown buildings and eyed him suspiciously as he passed, but he walked with purpose and kept his head down, and he felt their attention wane and shift away. Brennan soon arrived at his destination, a brightly lit building with glass double doors.

It was one of the chain convenience stores with a pharmacy in the rear corner. He entered and walked straight to the back, approaching the assistant at the counter.

"What can I do for you, sir?"

"Hey, I'm gonna need a patch of NicoClean."

"One patch?" the young pharmacist asked. "We only provide them in packs of fifteen and thirty."

"Fine," Brennan said. "Give me a fifteen-pack."

"I'll need your prescription first."

Brennan made a show of patting his pockets. "I don't have one of those." His hand slapped the wallet in his pocket and his eyes widened in mock surprise. He flipped it open and smacked it down on the counter, his silver badge showing prominently. "But hey, I've got this. Police business. Go get me a box."

"I—I don't know if I can do that," the pharmacist stammered.

"I'm a detective," Brennan said solemnly. "And you're about to be brought in for obstructing a police investigation."

"We have generic brands that you—" He was silenced by Brennan's glare. The young man gulped visibly, then turned and disappeared behind a shelf. A moment later, he returned with a box of NicoClean, one with thirty patches.

"Here you go," he said. "I'm not in any trouble, am I?"

"Not if you keep your nose clean and your head down." Brennan held his stare for a moment more, then retrieved his badge from the counter and stalked out of the pharmacy.

Once he was outside again, he stepped under the light of a streetlamp and looked critically at the box. It was standard in every way, with a Surgeon General's warning on the back. He broke the seal and took a single patch from the box; it was square-shaped, about the thickness of a credit card, and wrapped in clear plastic. It looked like any other patch.

So who would buy them in bulk? Brennan wondered. *And why kill the supplier?*

He put the patch in one of his pockets, then carried the box in one hand as he walked back toward the shuttle station. It was a quiet night; the moon was full and low on the horizon, and it inched its way over the city's towering skyline. A pair of cats were getting it on in an alley; he didn't care to look, and he quickened his pace a bit.

He wasn't paying attention when a lead pipe slammed him from behind.

It didn't *quite* hit his neck—the blow landed across his broad shoulders—but it hurt enough to stun him. He staggered forward and fell to the ground, his arms only partially absorbing the impact. A moment passed where he was kicked in the ribs and the box was ripped from his grasp, then he rolled to the side and lurched to his feet.

The lead pipe was wielded by a younger man with

a red and white Badgers cap, maybe in his late twenties. His partner, holding the box of NicoClean, circled around Brennan to flank him. Badgercap swung the lead pipe in his hand and lunged at Brennan with a savage cry.

Brennan took a glancing blow to the arm and spun with the swing of the pipe, grabbing the man by the wrist and hurling him bodily at his partner. The throw was poorly aimed, and the other man dodged as Badgercap flailed and nearly brained him with the lead pipe. He dropped the box of patches and brought his fists up to bear. His punches were direct and connected, but Brennan was a much larger man, and the blows caused bruises instead of broken bones. Brennan covered his head as the boxer tried to break through the defense, his fists landing on hard flesh and layered muscle.

Meanwhile, Brennan edged toward the rising moon.

If he could put himself between his attackers and the shuttle station, he could make a run for it. His size meant that fights tended to go in his favor, but he didn't like his chances going toe-to-toe with two prepared assailants. The lead pipe gave them a distinct advantage, too. His shoulders twinged painfully, and he couldn't raise his arms any higher than his face. He had to end this fight while Badgercap was still out of it.

He focused on the boxer and closed the distance. There was almost a rhythm to the punches, and he tried to gauge their timing. He took a blow high on his shoulder and closed to within inches, too close to be hit effectively. Brennan drove a knee into the man's groin, and the boxer's face twisted in agony. As he bent over protectively, Brennan brought his elbow down upon the man's neck, knocking him to the ground.

The lead pipe cracked across the back of Brennan's knees. His legs crumpled with a sickening pop, and he shouted out a curse. Pain coursed through his legs and his vision turned blood red. He was seeing scarlet as Badgercap lifted his beaten friend to his feet. He held the end of the lead pipe against Brennan's chest.

"I'm only going to say this once," Badgercap growled, his voice hoarse as he breathed heavily through his mouth. "Stay clear of Leviathan."

Brennan brushed the pipe away and received a blow to the head for it. The cold pipe pressed against his chest again.

"This doesn't have to be difficult," the armed man said. "Keep out of our business, and we will see that you are rewarded for your wise choice. I will not be so lenient next time." He paused to take a swift kick at Brennan's injured side. "Tell your partner, the little blonde chick, that *this* is a message. We've got our bases covered, and you've struck out."

He swung the lead pipe again, and Brennan saw stars.

He had been knocked Looney Tunes senseless, sure, but now he saw actual stars as he sprawled onto his back. Thousands upon thousands of blurry pinpoints of light suspended millions of miles away. They weren't supposed to be blurry, but his eyes refused to focus properly. His head was killing him, and he couldn't even lift his arms to cradle it. He could only listen with one good ear as Badgercap and his crony took off. They took the box of NicoClean with them.

Sometime later, he regained his sense of self. He could think clearly enough to know to get up. It was raining lightly. It must have been falling for a while now, since his clothes and jacket were plastered to his skin. He stood unsteadily and took quick steps to lean against the nearest lamppost. His ribs ached, and each intake of breath was fire in his chest. His shoulders were stiff as a corpse; he could barely lift his arms out straight, and shrugging would be a chore for the next few days. The sidewalk swayed beneath him as he walked like a drunkard down the street. The shuttle station lay ahead, and he knew where he had to go from there—if his body held together long enough.

CHAPTER FOURTEEN

AS WITH ANY garden, the most remarkable thing about the Jardin des Anges was its flowers.

Tourists came annually from all across the States to look upon the gardens. Every color imaginable was found in the petals of the Jardin, and the quietude created by the enclosure made it one of the most serene and romantic settings in the country. One could hardly walk along its cobbled lanes without being awestruck. A secret garden flourished when the winds were harshest and the temperature was at its lowest. It was for this reason that the Jardin had earned its name.

But the Jardin that Jeremy visited in his dream was its summery sister, the same one he had first witnessed in his father's memory.

He walked along the cobblestone paths with bare feet. They were smooth and cool to the touch, despite the warm sun high overhead. As he walked, his ankles were tickled by slender vines that had overgrown their assigned plots of land. He moved quietly among the peaceful gardens, and he soon found himself padding softly on an earthen path deep in the Jardin.

A jade beetle hummed its wings and flew across Jeremy's path, less than an inch from his face. He flinched away from it, and when he opened his eyes again, he saw an older gentleman turning the corner ahead and disappearing out of view.

It was odd, because there had been nobody in front of him a moment ago. He hurried after the man, and as he turned he saw a dark coattail flit around another corner. Jeremy followed the gentleman through the maze deeper into the Jardin, always a second too slow to see his face.

He paid no attention to where he was going until his feet landed upon solid stone. It was not the cobblestone of the earlier paths, nor the packed earth he had just left. Somehow, without realizing it, he had walked straight into some lower floor of the building that stood beside the Jardin.

"Old man!" he called. His voice echoed loud and long, and he flinched at the sudden idea that he might not be welcome here. "Old man," he said more quietly, addressing the nearby hallway juncture.

"I am not that old," came a reply.

A man of middling height, equal to Jeremy's own, stepped out from a connecting hallway. His hair was white and short around the temples, and deep grooves were worn into the fabric of his face. He was dressed to the nines, an impeccable suit that one might wear to the opera—if the performance were taking place a hundred years ago. His eyes were hidden by dark sunglasses and bushy eyebrows.

No way he ran that fast. Jeremy fought to catch his breath as he stared incredulously. The old man wasn't even winded.

"You have the most curious dreams," the man said without preamble, shifting his attention to look out the window.

Jeremy frowned. "What do you mean?"

"The Jardin des Anges. Beautiful place, just beautiful." The old man turned to stare directly at him. "But you have never been here."

Jeremy didn't know how to respond to that. It was true, but there was no way the old man could know. *He's a figment of your imagination,* one part of him rationalized, and he nodded. It made sense. But then why would he imagine this blind man?

"Your head," the man continued, "is so full of memories. Too full. How *ever* did you manage that?"

Jeremy was uncomfortable with this line of questioning. "Who are you?" he asked. "Have we met before?"

The old man barked out a laugh. "No," he said, "and I suppose this is all rather strange to you. I appear as I wish and I have many names. But you may call me Benjamin."

"All right, Ben. How did you get here?"

"I walked here, just as you did."

"Not the building," Jeremy said, frustrated. "I mean, how did you appear in my dream?"

"You know you are dreaming?" Benjamin asked. His white eyebrows raised slightly. "Few people are lucid dreamers."

Jeremy shrugged. "As you said, I've never been here before, and I'm *certainly* not here now."

"But your father has been here?" Benjamin asked.

He ignored the probing question. "You're changing the subject."

"As are you."

"Why are you here? Answer my question!"

"You are…*unique*, Jeremy."

He shivered at the sound of his name; he had never given it to the old man.

"You are unique," Benjamin continued, "just as I am. You ask who I am, and I will tell you." He moved in closer, and his voice dropped to a whisper. "I am a Sleeper."

If that simple statement was meant to unnerve

him, it worked. Sleepers were fairy tales, ghost stories, the kind of thing that little children played about because they were simply too unreal. The fable went that Sleepers could enter the dreams of anyone they wished, tormenting them or driving them to madness. Men with tinfoil hats claimed that there was a ward in the hospital for such Fractured minds.

If what Old Ben said was true, Jeremy was in deep trouble.

"I can see what you are thinking," the old man said softly. "And I must tell you that it is false, all of it. I am not the boogeyman come to steal your dreams, nor am I the maker of madmen. If it helps, you may think of us as the Dream Police."

Jeremy wasn't sure if he believed him. His heart calmed a little, though, and he had not yet run away from the man.

"You do not believe me," Benjamin said, seemingly reading his thoughts. "I do not blame you. Perhaps a demonstration is in order?"

Before Jeremy could say another word, the floor and walls shook violently around them. Ancient dust shifted loose from the ceiling overhead, and the stones that formed the foundation of the wall vibrated dangerously in place. It was like a great, rumbling earthquake had suddenly overtaken the Jardin des Anges, prepared to swallow them up in an instant.

With sickening abruptness, they were no longer in that stretch of hallway.

Jeremy looked out over a field of peonies, a green landscape dotted with innumerable blooms of pink and red and orange. The flowers swayed in the gentle breeze, and he smelled their collective aroma carried on the wind.

"We use our power for good, Jeremy." The field of flowers disappeared in a blur of colors, as if Van Gogh were given free rein of this ride, and the two of them were suddenly standing aboard one of the shuttles, back in Odols. There was only one other man sitting in the car, and he was bleeding from a cut on his lip. "But there are few of us, and the darkness grows," Benjamin continued. "Odols is not as safe of a city as it once was. It is time to recruit, and I am here for you."

Another disorienting shift in the world, and they now stood in the hallway once more, only a few feet apart. Jeremy could see the heavy lines of Ben's face even more clearly. They were the marks of a hard life, one fraught with danger and darkness...

And purpose.

"Who was that man?" Jeremy asked.

"A former agent of mine, turned away from our order by doubt and selfish desires." Benjamin peered at him through the dark glasses as if he could see perfectly well. "These are not traits that I sense in you."

"You want me…to be like you? To become a Sleeper?"

"Not right away," Old Ben said. "There will be years before that is necessary. You are yet uneducated, untrained. I am simply here to tell you that, when your schooling is finished, you have a place here." Silence hung in the air between them for several seconds.

"You said that I was special *like you*," Jeremy said slowly. "How are you special?"

"I do not speak lightly of what I can do," Benjamin said curtly. "It is a valuable asset. It is why *you* have not yet acknowledged what you are capable of."

"Fair enough. Truth for truth?"

Benjamin nodded. "Trust is a bridge that extends both ways."

"Fine." Jeremy took a deep breath and let it out slowly. "I can…see other people's memories. Kind of like I'm downloading their entire lives into my brain."

The pinched lines around Benjamin's eyes sharpened. "As I suspected."

"You already knew?" he asked incredulously.

"The last time you fell asleep, your dreams lit up like a beacon. You have so very, *very* many memories in that head. When that kind of number is accumulated, the memories are usually fuzzy and gray, aged alongside the person who holds them. But yours…"

Ben said, waving a finger. "Each one of yours was crisp and fresh, like a freshly fallen autumn leaf. And so *vivid*. They were as new to you as breakfast this morning. It was this anomaly that attracted me," he said simply.

The two of them stood in silence for what seemed like an eternity. Dream time moved very differently from waking time. Their entire conversation could have taken place in the first few moments of him passing out in bed.

"And how are you special?" Jeremy finally asked. Old Ben shrugged.

"I am a Pathfinder. I find things, and people."

"And paths?"

Benjamin laughed. "Exactly."

Jeremy asked the question that had been on his mind since the Tower. "How can I do what I do? What made me get like this?"

"You make it sound like a disease," Benjamin said. His eyebrows knitted together into a solid line. "Nobody knows for certain what sets us apart. The hand of God? A mutation in our genes?"

"But I haven't always been like this," Jeremy protested. "All of this started when I hit my head a couple days ago. Could brain trauma be the cause of all this? Am I just imagining everything in my head?"

Old Ben smiled wanly. "I should hope not, or else I might find myself quoting the late Albus

Dumbledore."

"He's a fictional character."

"Yes, a figment of one author's imagination. Why should that make him any less real?" He smiled ruefully. "You forced my hand."

Jeremy didn't smile. "You still haven't told me anything. Why are we like this?"

Benjamin shrugged. "Why does it matter? We are who we are, whether by another's hand or our own. Scores of men have searched their entire lives for the meaning of life, the *why*, and many more have quested after the *how*." He folded his hands over his cane. "I am content with knowing that I *am*."

Jeremy digested the old man's words. "And everyone who is a Sleeper, they're all special like us?"

"Not everyone," Benjamin said. "There are others with powers such as ours, though they are few in number. Any individual with sufficient willpower could learn to do what Sleepers do. But *our* abilities appear to be from a different set of gifts entirely."

"Finding things…forgive me for saying so, but that doesn't sound like such a great gift."

"We do not choose the gifts we are given," Benjamin said. "In any case, I found you."

Jeremy lifted his chin. "I'm a beacon. That's different."

"Do not let your head swell too big for your

shoulders."

"So what exactly would I do as a Sleeper? I've heard only bad things, and that was when I still thought you were a bedtime story. If even half of it is true—"

"We do what is necessary to protect this city," Benjamin said tightly. "There are forces that are simply too powerful and mysterious to be handled by the police. We are the self-appointed protectors of the people."

"That's a great pitch, but I meant day-to-day, *what will I be doing?*"

Old Ben seemed to contemplate this question for a long moment before answering. "There is no right or wrong in this world, Jeremy. You must understand that in order to bring balance to others, we must first find balance within ourselves. This will not be an easy life, nor one filled with thanks from those you help—they will never even know you were there. You will make hard choices, decisions that will leave others bereft of their autonomy. But with my guiding hand, you will accomplish great deeds and protect countless innocents during your service."

"That still doesn't answer—"

"You will kill. You will maim. You will steal, lie, and deceive. Nobody will know who you are, or what you do, or when or where you will strike next. It is a dangerous life, but one that is necessary for the continued survival of this city. The people will never acknowledge your sacrifices, and they will continue to fear and despise the myth that you represent."

There was a pregnant pause before Benjamin spoke again.

"Do you have what it takes?" he asked.

Jeremy stared at him for a long moment. "You need to work on your sales pitch."

"It is not typical for so many questions to be asked so early on." Benjamin's head tilted as he seemed to consider something off to the side. "I fear I must be going now. Time is short, and I have many more to contact before the night is through. It was a pleasure to make your acquaintance, Collector."

Jeremy frowned at the title, but he decided not to ask any more questions. He felt Benjamin had told him all he would. "Nice meeting you, too, Benjamin."

"I hope you do give serious consideration to what we discussed here." He rapped his cane lightly against the stone floor. "You will make a fine Sleeper one day."

Jeremy nodded. "Put me down as a definite maybe. Though I'll have to ask my parents about it."

"This is not something you ask permission to do. This is something you are *born* to do." The old man started to leave, but stopped mid-turn and glanced at Jeremy again. "I would have that wound tended to by a doctor, if I were you," he advised.

As Benjamin walked away, the walls of the building around them didn't crumble so much as waver out of existence, gradually being replaced with the wood and glass of Jeremy's bedroom. The old man turned a corner, and a door materialized behind him, completing the room's transformation.

Damn, he's good, Jeremy thought.

ф ф ф

THERE WERE NO voices in the room when Jeremy came to. The fireplace was lit once more across the room, and the heavy blankets that had been lain upon him were still smothering. But this time he did not wake to pain and misery; his head hurt, but only a little, and he felt perfectly rested, as if he had not just spent the entire night speaking with Old Ben in his dream.

And he hadn't. He looked outside to see the night barely half spent, the moon hanging high in the sky as if at the peak of a rollercoaster, poised for its inevitable descent. It was full and bright, lighting the whole valley in dull gray and blue accented here and there by lingering shadows.

He pulled himself from beneath the covers and put on a fresh set of clothes. Voices carried from the kitchen, and he walked out to investigate. His mother, father, and uncle were all seated around the table, talking and laughing animatedly.

"Look who woke from the dead!" boomed Uncle Rick. Jeremy's parents hushed the boisterous man, and Annabelle glanced at the closed door to Ellie's room. His sister must have fallen asleep hours ago. "How are you feeling?" his uncle asked in a quieter voice.

"Pretty good," he admitted, rolling his shoulders. "I'm starving."

"We saved you some dinner, sweetie," his mother said, rising from her chair. She gestured for him to sit down while she heated a bowl of leftover stew over the stove.

"And after that," Nathaniel said, "you're going straight back to bed."

"Oh, come now," Uncle Rick argued. "He's been asleep all evening. Let the boy stay up with the adults for once."

"I'm not a boy," Jeremy said quietly.

"I'm sorry, of course you aren't," Uncle Rick said, throwing him a jovial wink with his apology. Jeremy smiled, and his mother brought over a steaming bowl of stew. She also set down a glass of water and painkillers.

"Thanks, Mom."

"Careful, it's hot."

"You don't need to coddle him," Uncle Rick chided before focusing on Jeremy. "I was just telling your father here that we should open up the valley."

"Open up the valley?"

"Yessir, bring in some developers and make a resort hotel out here. Maybe some camping grounds, for hikers and the like. Some people will pay a small fortune to have a getaway location like this, even for a week or two. We'd become barons of our own piece of paradise," he said, laughing deeply.

"It isn't *your* land to develop," Annabelle said sternly. "Ultimately, the decision rests with Nate."

"You're right, of course, Anna," he said, his tone placating. "But I would stay on as an adviser, naturally, providing my expertise for rolling everything out."

"And what exactly do you know about running a resort hotel?"

Uncle Rick raised his shoulders and said, "What can I tell you? I've been around a lot. I know what a good place looks like and how it should run. With an opportunity like this, you'll recoup your investment in just a few years, and then it's all profit." He ruffled Jeremy's hair. "Investment for this guy and Ellie to live off of when they are older."

"This *valley* is their inheritance," Nathaniel interjected. "All of this land, this fresh, fertile, *clean* land, will be theirs one day."

"I'm not saying we should pollute it—just the opposite, in fact! We're offering a place for city-dwellers to escape all the smog and traffic. Everybody wants to get away once in a while, and we'd offer the full package. You aren't using this whole valley, anyway. Not even a twentieth of it. The rest is potential profit, unrealized returns."

Jeremy could see his father smiling now at the opportunity. His mother, though still uncertain, looked less upset than she had earlier. A sudden thought occurred to him.

"We could rebuild the Tower!" he blurted out.

Uncle Rick gave him a look. "The tower?" he asked.

His father waved a dismissive hand. "It's a rundown old building that Jeremy ran off to alone." He stared hard at Jeremy. "That place is a death trap. It nearly got him killed."

"Boys will be boys," Rick said with a laugh, but the joke fell flat. He looked compromisingly between Jeremy and Nathaniel. "We can rebuild it," he said, "and improve upon it to make it a proper building, with all the safety regulations you could wish for. We can set out for it first thing."

"Maybe now isn't the best time to be discussing this," Annabelle said, getting up from the table.

Uncle Rick placed both hands flat on the table. "Right. Best save the details for tomorrow, when we're all rested and ready to begin."

"Yes," she sighed. "That's exactly what I meant."

Nathaniel rose as well, brushing her cheek with his lips as she walked toward the bedroom.

Uncle Rick looked at his brother with a wide, toothy smile. "You know this is the right thing to do," he said in his baritone voice.

Nathaniel's face broke out in a grin at his brother's words. "I know it is, of course." He pointed a thumb at Jeremy's retreating mother. "Somebody still needs a little convincing, though. I'll see you in the morning. Come on, son, let's get you to bed."

He placed a hand on Jeremy's shoulder and the two of them walked back down the hallway. The fire crackled merrily, and Jeremy was reluctant to get back under the stifling bedcovers. He sat on top while his father rested on the edge of the bed. Nathaniel had gentle lines in his face, premature aging brought about by stress. The gray in his temples grew a little bit each day, accentuating his gray eyes more and more.

"Jay," he began, "I know I haven't been the best father to you. I've said this all before, but you need to hear it again, because I truly mean it." He bit his cheek, an unfamiliar gesture. Jeremy felt something stir inside that he had never felt for his father before. He flashed back to the memory of his father, as a young boy, sitting in that rundown apartment.

"You're doing the best you can for us," Jeremy

said quietly. "Nobody blames you for not wanting to be like your father."

Nathaniel looked at his son for a second, then let out a quiet laugh.

"Sometimes I forget how much you've grown," he said. "You're practically an adult now."

"Practically?" Jeremy asked, eyebrow raised.

His father laughed again. "Don't grow up too fast," he said, slinging one arm around Jeremy's shoulders. They sat together in a companionable silence for several seconds, then a few minutes. Neither one moved from the half-embrace. From the living room, the grandfather clock tolled twice before falling silent again. "You really want that old fort rebuilt?" he asked.

Jeremy sat back then and looked at his father. Those eyes were worried, and calculating, and loving. The three would have seemed incongruent in another man, but Jeremy acknowledged that his father wasn't just any other man. He was the one who had looked out for him his whole life, working himself to the bone and nearly losing his marriage so that his children wouldn't grow up as he had. Jeremy recognized that now, just as he recognized that this offer was one of reconciliation with his father.

He nodded. "Yeah. That's what I want."

Nathaniel nodded. "Then that's how we'll do it.

I'll let your uncle know in the morning."

"And Dad?"

"Yes, Jay?"

Jeremy bit his lip. "How did you...why was there already a doctor here for when we returned?"

Nathaniel wringed his hands together as his face fell. His eyes held the saddest expression Jeremy had ever seen, and there was a somber tone to his voice when he spoke. "Jay, I'm...I wanted to have everyone's blood drawn for a routine checkup."

Jeremy could hear the lie in his father's voice, but he wasn't sure why it was there. "Why do you need our blood?"

"Just making sure that everything is fine. Can never be too careful, right?"

"I suppose not..."

Nathaniel patted Jeremy on the arm before standing and going to the door. "Time for bed, all right? I'm glad you're well," he said sincerely. "I'll see you in the morning."

CHAPTER FIFTEEN

BRENNAN WAS VERY close to passing out on the shuttle.

It was dark now that he was underground, and the rhythmic motion of the shuttle and its low, constant hum were lulling him to sleep. He took ragged breaths and scowled each time one of the tunnel lights passed by the window. They were too bright and only served to worsen his headache. He was contemplating going comatose—which seemed like a really good option at the moment—when his phone vibrated in his pocket.

Thankfully, his arms could still move in the downward direction, though it was a chore bringing it close enough to his ear to hear.

"Brennan," he rasped.

"Did I wake you?" It was a female voice. Bishop.

"No, actually, just about to fall asleep. What's

up?"

"You sound terrible, or maybe it's just the reception."

"Both," he said dryly. "I'm on the shuttle home now from uptown. Oh, and I got jumped."

"What?" Alarm colored her voice. "You were attacked? By who?"

Brennan shrugged, then regretted it. Fire seared across his shoulders, and Bishop couldn't see the gesture at any rate. He hissed in discomfort.

"Brennan?"

"I'm fine," he told her. False. "Two guys, one had a Badgers cap and a lead pipe." He lifted his chin slightly. "They ran, in the end."

Bishop's voice was apprehensive. "Well, all right. Glad to hear you came out on top. Who would attack a cop?"

"Don't know. Guess they were watching the pharmacy. They mentioned you, by the way. We're supposed to stay away from the Nettle murder."

He heard a snort through the receiver. "Yeah, like that's going to happen," Bishop said. He felt his lower lip crack with a sharp burst of discomfort, but the grin was worth it.

"All the same, this case is getting more dangerous. We should probably check things out together from now on." His nephew's drug-induced vision suddenly came to mind. He thought about telling Bishop what Greg had seen, but then decided against it. She would dismiss it as nonsense and possibly bring Greg up on drug charges, to boot.

"Hello?"

Brennan had lost the thread of conversation. "I'm sorry, uh, connection must have dropped out. What did you say?"

"I said I called because they found out something new about our body during the autopsy."

"Oh? What's that?"

"You remember the irritation we saw around the eyes?" Brennan shuddered at the mental image of the horribly mutilated eye sockets. "Wallace's report just came in: the redness we saw was deteriorated tissue caused by the corrosive substances in patches."

"Patches?" Brennan echoed. The single NicoClean patch he had removed from the box was still in his pocket. He was definitely not going to mention Greg's patch problem.

"Yeah, that psychoactive drug that's giving the boys in vice such a hard time. Damn hallucinogens. It's not what killed him, but Nettle was alive long enough for the patches to take effect."

Brennan felt bile rise in his throat. "And some sick bastard put a patch on each eye. Zachariah must've been in agony right until he bled out."

His partner's voice wavered slightly. "We're hunting a psychopath."

ɸ ɸ ɸ

IT WAS JUST past three in the morning when Brennan stumbled into the precinct.

He was the definition of misery. Every bone in his body ached, and he hadn't had a decent sleep in days. Hell, the last time he'd slept, he'd relived the worst moment of his life and a Sleeper had tried to put a bullet between his eyes. Alarms were blaring in his head, warning him that something was messed up inside him, urging him to go home. He lived on the same block; all he had to do was cross the street.

But he didn't. As much as his body longed for rest, he still had a job to do. Once, long ago, he could have gone home to a wife, slept easy at night, and come back in the morning. It was a sweet memory, tinged with bitterness with the knowledge that he could never again lay claim to that kind of happiness. Now, the job was all he had, all he could do.

The precinct was brightly lit, even at this hour, and Brennan scowled in protest. His feet shuffled past a concerned-looking receptionist and he thumbed the button for the elevator. It was only one floor to the morgue, but he doubted his ability to tackle stairs at the moment. Bishop was waiting for him with the evening pathologist when he reached the basement. She nodded her greeting, and Brennan nodded back.

"Brennan," he grunted to the pathologist, offering a hand.

"Wallace. We've met before, actually," he said, taking the handshake politely.

"Have we?" Brennan squinted through bleary eyes at the unfamiliar man. He was a slender man of Indian descent, and he was short for a grown man, almost of a height with Bishop. A single line of jet-black hair led from his forehead to the base of his neck. Studded piercings gleamed from both ears. The three of them started walking to the morgue proper, a large, sterile room that dominated three quarters of the basement.

"At the policemen's banquet two years ago," Wallace supplied. "You and Sam were working on the Red Eye murders then."

"Sorry, Wally," Brennan mumbled. "It's been kind of a long day, and I'm bad with faces."

"Wallace is just my last name, actually. My first name is—"

"Brennan, you said you were fine." Bishop gave him a concerned glance.

"—Jeffrey."

"I've never felt stronger. And I think 'Wally'

sounds better."

"Well I—"

"You shouldn't be here," Bishop protested. "If I'd known you were coming in such shit condition, I wouldn't have called."

"Maybe we should—"

"I've run longer on less. I can sleep when I'm dead."

"Probably not the best euphemism to use in the morgue."

"Detectives!" Wally had stopped dead in his tracks. "It's late, we're all tired, and there's a sadistic drug dealer-turned-murderer running around! A little focus, please!"

The two detectives glanced at one another, then followed the pathologist in silence. Brennan did what he could to hide his limp, and Bishop reined in her concern.

Wally led them to the too-pale corpse of Zachariah Nettle laying on a slab of cold metal. His big toe had a small yellow tag looped around it, and a folded surgical towel covered him sensibly. The cavities left in his face where his eyes had been removed looked more garish now than they had a few days ago. They were deep, sunken pits that added purple to the mottled red and yellow of his visage. The chemical burns on the skin around the eye sockets were turning a sickly brown color in some places.

"Always a shame to lose a professional peer," Wally sighed. "Not a pathologist, mind you, but trained in medicine all the same." He turned to the other two with an upturned mouth. "We medics patch you up and get you on your way with hardly any thanks in return."

Brennan raised an eyebrow. "What'chu talkin' 'bout, Wallace?"

Bishop snorted, then turned it into a cough.

"You work with dead people," Brennan continued. "And Nettle filled prescription bottles."

"At least you got my name right," Wally grumbled before regaining his composure. "Medicine is indistinguishable from poison when administered improperly. Do you know how many bodies I have coming through here because they OD'd on what should have been life-preserving medicine? Take our victim, for instance. What would you say is the active ingredient in patches?"

The two detectives shared a glance.

"It's a name too long for you to understand even if I told you," Wally continued. "But the common name is Chamalla."

"I thought there wasn't enough viable tissue left to sample," Brennan said skeptically.

"I'm better than most," Wally said with a smirk.

"It's corrosive, right? Bleeds right through the epidermis. There was too little surface tissue, sure, but there was more than enough to sample beneath the skin."

Brennan grunted. "Clever. So what is Chamalla?"

"Once upon a time, it was thought to be an alternative cure for cancer. They did a whole miniseries about it, but it was eventually debunked. Instead of tossing the project, other applications were looked into. It showed promise in treating patients with Alzheimer's. You know how memory works as you get older?"

They really didn't, but neither detective interrupted the pathologist.

"New memories accumulate over time and older, less important memories are stored away. Not gone, not like we used to think, but put away somewhere. Just like how you put Christmas ornaments in the basement when you aren't using them," he clarified, his eyes hopeful.

Bishop nodded politely, while Brennan stood stone-faced. He didn't know anybody in the city who had a basement.

"Right. Well just like that, you still have all your memories, they're just put away somewhere that you don't think about, or else it's just difficult to reach. They say that every person you see in your dreams is someone you've actually seen in real life, but I think that's bogus. Since you don't remember every single thing you've done in your life, your brain creates filler material for the parts you no longer remember. Over time, this filler material accumulates and can take on a life of its own, and so we get elderly patients who remember an entire life that never happened."

"Kind of running away from us here, Wally," Brennan warned. "Is there a shorter explanation?"

Wally looked at Brennan and Bishop alternately with the strangest expression on his face. Disappointment, perhaps, that they weren't as engrossed in all the details as he was.

He cleared his throat. "Right. Anyway, this medicine, Chamalla, clears away all the filler. Or it should, anyway. I've never used it myself, personally." Heat suddenly entered Wally's voice as he gestured to Nettle's body. "But then someone decided to take that medicine, crank up the dosage to insane levels, and sell it on the streets as dope—"

The drug was medicine. Brennan's mind was fuzzy, as if the gears were trying to turn with gum jammed up in the works. Bishop had no such trouble thinking clearly.

"You're saying the drug is medicine, but used improperly, is that it?"

Wally was still in his own rant. "—and they add to

it with chemicals and narcotics and—sorry, what? Oh, yes. Of course," he said, looking at her as if she were a simpleton.

"How much more Chamalla would you need to use to go from medicinal to recreational?" she asked.

"Not much," Wally said. "The difference is in milliliters."

"Why do the patches burn the applied surface? This is supposed to be medicine, after all."

"All things in moderation. Remember, they were trying to use this stuff to treat cancer. The alternative was blasting the cells with radiation, and we know the kind of toll that takes on the body. Considering the options, the toxicity of the extract was deemed acceptable. In small doses, it works wonders on our Alzheimer's patients. With an increased dosage, you would start to run into the more toxic side of things."

Wally touched the cold body for a moment, gingerly, on the head. "It's really ingenious," he said, "using the patches as an application method. Slow, steady release of the drug, and the epidermis takes most of the blow instead of the internal organs. If—when—you catch our culprit, I would love to have a few minutes to discuss his thought process."

"But Wally—er, Wallace," Bishop corrected herself at his sharp glance. "The patches are practically worthless. Why kill the pharmacist supplying patches when the Chamalla is what is worth killing somebody over?"

Brennan's brain finally made connection with his mouth. "There are two points of vulnerability," he said.

"What do you mean?" Bishop asked.

"I'm...not sure." He didn't quite understand the words himself. He shivered in his still-damp clothes, and something shifted in his pocket. Brennan reached a hand inside and felt the square shape of the NicoClean patch. He pulled it out absentmindedly.

"The men who jumped me," he said. "They were prepared by the time I came snooping around. One of them told me that they 'had their bases covered.'"

"Which meant they were watching the pharmacy," Bishop concluded.

"No, no," he said, waving a hand. "I think he slipped up. You said it yourself, there are two aspects of the patch: the physical patch itself, and the Chamalla. I think when he said bases, plural, that it meant they have something—or someone—else under their control."

Bishop put two and two together. "They need to be getting their supply of Chamalla from somewhere."

"When we kept visiting the pharmacy, they must have thought we already knew about the role of the prescription patches in Zachariah Nettle's murder and that we planned on shutting down the operation. By running us off, they could move back in and press somebody else under their thumb." Brennan thought of how easily the other pharmacist had rolled under his pressure, and he had barely even been trying. "We need to solve this soon," he said, "before they draw in anybody else."

Bishop faced Brennan squarely, hands on her hips, her mouth set in a stern frown. "We aren't going to keep them from rolling on Nettle's pharmacy?"

Brennan shook his head. "If we stay there, they'll just move to another pharmacy. The patches are easy, and it would be impossible to cover every store that sells them. There can only be a handful of places that can supply the amount of Chamalla that they need, though. If we hit their source of the drug, we'll put them out of business."

"This is so cool," Wally said, watching the exchange with wide eyes.

Brennan placed the damp NicoClean patch over one of the corpse's empty eye sockets; its edges lined up neatly with the red, ruined skin.

Bishop made a sign of the cross.

CHAPTER SIXTEEN

WHEN THE SUN rose, it did so in secret.

Thick clouds, dark and foreboding, moved in from the west and settled over the valley. The light drizzle of the night before had been replaced by a steady downpour that hammered against the roof and drenched the valley. Every so often, the fabric of the sky would be torn asunder by a bolt of fire, followed by the beat of a god's drum that left the earth trembling. Wind howled outside the Scott ranch like a horde of banshees.

Storms like these were not infrequent in the Midwest, and each time one came along, it was a terrible thing to behold.

"Out of nowhere!" Uncle Rick remarked, his loud voice managing to rise over the cacophony around them. Though it was impossible to tell by looking at the sky, it was midmorning, and everybody was gathered around the table for breakfast. His father and Uncle Rick had been talking about their plans to renovate the valley when Jeremy joined them, though that conversation fell quiet when his mother emerged from his parents' bedroom. The topic had abruptly shifted to the weather.

"Oh, please," Annabelle said. "You two don't fool me for a second. Go on talking about whatever it is I interrupted," she added, feigning indifference.

It's a trap! Jeremy mouthed, and his uncle hid a smile behind a napkin as he pretended to dab at his mouth.

"I have never seen such temperamental weather," Uncle Rick blustered. He gestured at the rain that pelted against the windows; pellets of hail had joined the mix. "Sunny just yesterday, without a cloud in the sky! A light drizzle last night, sure, but this is just obscene!"

"Come on, Derrick," his father said. "You're exaggerating now. You've been all around the globe! A little rain isn't anything new to you."

"This is not *a little rain*." Uncle Rick shook his head. "You Midwesterners."

"You were born here, too, you know."

He ignored Nathaniel's comment. "One time," Uncle Rick began, looking between Ellie and Jeremy,

"I was in South America, in Brazil. The climate down there is damp. Humid. The clothes were clinging to my back, but my sweat must have smelled like honey, because we were getting bitten left and right by mosquitoes. The air was so thick with them that we couldn't open our mouths, in case we accidentally swallowed one."

"Eww!" Ellie exclaimed, wrinkling her nose.

Uncle Rick laughed. "It's true! My buddy Jimmy and I, we shed all but our lightest fatigues, and there was still no respite from the heat."

"Fatigues? You were never in any military," Annabelle argued.

"We were dressed as local militia," he confided, "so we had to look the part. Anyway, we were lost and dying of thirst. The closest town was over thirty miles away through dense rainforest." Jeremy opened his mouth to talk, but his uncle overrode him. "I can guess what you're thinking: we were in the rainforest, so there was water everywhere for us to drink. But there wasn't."

Uncle Rick licked his lips, the phantom sensation of thirst apparently getting to him. "We were *disguised* as local militia, but the men we encountered were nothing but thugs, men who offered their 'protection' services and burned down entire villages if people refused. Their boss was a drug lord dealing mostly with heroin, and—"

"I don't think this is a story you should be telling the kids," Annabelle said, frowning.

"But he was just getting to the good part," Jeremy pleaded.

His sister echoed him. "Yeah, the good part!"

"Ellie, you're definitely too young to hear this." Annabelle looked sharply at Uncle Rick. "Another time in more adult company, perhaps."

Her tone would brook no argument. Ellie protested by refusing to eat the rest of her breakfast, which would only make her more irritable later when she got hungry. Jeremy had finished eating by then, as had his father and uncle, and they excused themselves quietly from the table.

"Breakfast was delicious, thanks, honey," Nathaniel said, kissing his wife on the cheek.

Uncle Rick mirrored the gesture, and a peculiar expression flashed across Annabelle's face. 'Pleasant surprise' was how Jeremy would have described it. Everybody helped clear the table, with the exception of Ellie, who stalked off to her room.

"She adores his tales," Nathaniel said.

Annabelle accepted his dirty plate. "She's too young for that kind of story," she insisted.

Nathaniel nodded. "You're right, there. But Jeremy isn't."

She vigorously scrubbed the plate clean before placing it in the drying rack with a little more force than was necessary.

Jeremy listened discreetly; he had his face turned toward the window, as if he were wholly focused on the tempest outside. His face gave no indication otherwise; he had long ago learned the art of eavesdropping.

He found it difficult to think of them as Mom and Dad anymore. Ever since he had absorbed their memories—a fact which still freaked him out—he remembered every moment of both their lives with crystal clarity and surround sound. They had been together since their time at the university, and to each other they were simply Annabelle and Nathaniel. Jeremy rubbed at his uninjured temple. The memories were affecting his own perception of them as well. And then there were the nightmares.

For the past two nights, he had had cripplingly terrifying dreams. He never remembered what they were when he woke up—not like he remembered his encounter with Old Ben—but rather they left a kind of psychic scar. Sometimes, he had difficulty reaching a memory of his father's, or he couldn't recall a particular day in his mother's life. They were little things, the kind of absence that would go unnoticed over a lifetime. But he, Jeremy, who had taken in those lifetimes in a matter of seconds, saw them as clearly as missing pieces from a jigsaw puzzle.

Somehow, whatever he had done to absorb his parents' memories had been incomplete.

The scarred memories lived out their existence in forgotten dreams, though; his unconscious mind suffered each night from whatever horror resided in those missing moments. And each morning, he awoke with an awful feeling inside, like a sickness in his heart.

Even now, as he watched the rain fall and listened in on his parents' now idle chit-chat, he felt the phantom memories.

He looked across the room at Uncle Rick, who reclined easily in a chair that was decidedly *not* facing one of the windows. He considered taking his uncle's memories, too, but quickly decided against it. There was already too much to absorb right now; between his father, his mother, and himself, he had almost a solid century of memories. No wonder he had stood out so clearly to the Sleeper.

Jeremy bit his lip. Old Ben was a mystery, too. Jeremy had never given much consideration of what to do after high school; he had assumed that the university would be the next logical step for him, just as his parents had done. But what if that wasn't the case?

What if my destiny is to become a Sleeper?

He frowned. When he was younger, Sleepers had always been the boogeymen. Every child in Odols grew up with that belief. Over the years, he had come to know them as a make-believe tale, something told to children to make them behave, similar to Santa giving coal to those on his naughty list. If the encounter last night was any indication, Jeremy realized, it meant that his entire upbringing had been a lie. Sleepers were real, and they were keepers of the peace.

Old Ben had offered him the chance to be an agent for good in Odols. By operating in the shadows, never mentioned outside of old wives' tales, the Sleepers were rendered all the more effective.

The aching in his head returned. He didn't mention it outwardly to his family, especially not after the fainting episode from last night, but he felt their eyes watching as he abruptly left his spot by the window. He thought about grabbing a few painkillers before heading back to bed to sleep out the storm, but it would have only confirmed their suspicions. He gritted his teeth and walked straight to his room. He threw a log on the fireplace and it fell with a burst of sparks before slowly catching flame. Within minutes, the room was dry and warm from the crackling fire as a deluge poured down just outside.

He looked at the summer reading book that he had set aside on the table. It was still open to the first page, face down, just as he had left it. Near it was a small stack of other books, also on the reading list, none of which Jeremy had bothered to open. Now he had no need; they had all been read before by either Annabelle or Nathaniel. There was something conspicuously off about the surface of his reading table, though, and it took Jeremy a moment to realize what was different.

The sheet of paper on which he had written his father's signature was missing.

It wasn't hidden beneath any of the books, nor had an errant gust of wind blown it to the floor. It was simply gone. Neither hidden nor misplaced, there was only one other option: it had been taken. Jeremy's stomach pooled in his feet. His parents had been in here last night after his collapse; surely his father must have seen the paper. Would they suspect it had been a simple forgery? He had done it before for class field trips. It had its flaw, of course, with the awkward ending to the double-T that deviated from his father's muscle memory signature.

But then where was the paper now? And why had it not been mentioned at breakfast?

Chapter Seventeen

Noel walked Brennan across the street to his apartment and shoved him firmly onto the bed.

"To be honest," he said, "I'm half-hoping this is heading in the direction it looks like."

She punched him on the shoulder, and it wasn't gentle. "You're a pig." He tried to rise, but she pushed him down again until he was resting against the pillow. It felt like an angel's bosom beneath his head.

Brennan patted the open space next to him. "You're welcome to join."

Bishop cocked an eyebrow. "I think not," she said flatly.

"Sorry," he slurred. "Get tired when I'm weird." He frowned. "Wait, that didn't come out right."

"I understood what you meant," she said, smiling slightly before her expression sobered. "The answer is

139

still no. Sleep now. You haven't had a decent night's rest since this all started."

It had been years, actually, but he thought it best not to correct her. The bedspread was heavy and warm, especially since he still wore all his clothes from the previous day.

Bishop laid a hand on his arm. "Sam told me you've been having nightmares," she said gently. "And there's broken glass all over your living room floor." He began to protest, but she held up a hand. "I'm not looking for an explanation. Not yet, in any case. But if you're having any kind of trouble, I'm here to listen. That's what partners are for."

Brennan looked at her through heavy-lidded eyes. They had spent the dark hours of the morning working side-by-side, narrowing down the list of places where Chamalla shipments could be unloaded. Long hours passed during the tedious work, and by the time the rain started to fall in earnest it was a miracle either of them had managed to stay awake through it all. Brennan suspected he might have nodded off on one or more occasions.

The short walk from the precinct to his apartment had left them both drenched. He had already been thoroughly damp even before their conversation with Wally, so the downpour was only an unfortunate escalation for him; Bishop was completely unprepared for the state she now found herself in. Heavy rain fell outside even as she sat on the edge of his bed. He rose feebly, and she pushed him down again. "Sleep," she said firmly.

He couldn't tell her what was troubling him. Not yet, anyhow. But he also wasn't about to make her trudge home in the rain. "Aye aye, cap'n," he replied. He mumbled slightly, and the muscles that kept his eyes open had already decided to shut down. "There's a couch," he said lamely, gesturing blindly with one arm.

"Why, yes, I believe there is," he heard Bishop reply.

"Sleep," he suggested, as much to her as to himself.

He felt the bed shift as she stood, and a second later heard the bedroom door close softly behind her as she left. His body was spent, and he could feel the long pull of sleep tugging at him from not too far away. Still, he didn't want to ruin his bed with wet clothes, and the fix would take less than a minute.

Wearily, he freed himself from the comforter and stood up abruptly before he could change his mind. His fingers worked clumsily to unbutton his dress shirt, and he had to peel it off one sleeve at a time. The same went for his pants, which clung tightly against his thighs. Finally, he divested himself of the last bit of clothing he had on and collapsed back into bed. He had barely rotated into position and lain his head on the pillow when he was transported to another place.

φ φ φ

THE ROOM WAS wide enough to fit two buses side by side, and large, ornate crystal chandeliers hung on long chains of copper from the vaulted ceiling far above. The walls were adorned with blurred portraits of men and women with firm jaws and narrow noses, wearing clothes that dated back gradually through the centuries; some were as far back as the Old World, across the Atlantic.

Brennan stood upon an expansive tile mosaic of black and gold and white. The tiles were irregularly shaped and, seen from where he stood, were arranged in a way that formed a symbol in the floor, but its shape was unknown to him. Brennan's mouth opened in a small circle. He recognized the hall of the mansion he had once called home.

"Just when I thought I was out," he muttered.

The portraits on the walls resolved into the distinct faces of Brennan's ancestors. Short tables were spaced along the walls as well, topped with doilies and vases that were worth more than what he now earned in a year.

The hall, large enough to host a hundred people—as it once had on numerous occasions—was eerily deserted.

Brennan descended a curved marble staircase and pushed open a heavy door of solid oak, entering into one of the adjacent rooms. It was smallish, dimly lit, and a hazy smoke hung lazily in the air. A single light hung over a green felt pool table. The smoke had a rich scent to it, and Brennan had a fleeting sense of nostalgia as he inhaled. This was his father's office.

Brennan had never been allowed to enter during his father's meetings, and so he had had no idea as a child what sort of treachery the man was up to. On one occasion, he had barged in by accident, unaware of a meeting in progress. He had been greeted by empty stares and an ugly scowl from one of the men, a large brute with a scar over one eye. The younger version of himself had been terrified, though the man was far less intimidating in retrospect. He had almost certainly not been a rival of Brennan's own current size, and being half-blind could only have been a hindrance to him.

In fact, as a cop, he now saw the entire room in a different light.

There was a surprising amount of malice hanging in the air. Perhaps as a child, that had been what unconsciously kept him from entering the room. The smoke was not only hazy, but it was also thick and cloying; in the small confines of the room, it was suffocating. But his father was nowhere to be seen.

Brennan left the room and wandered around the rest of the house, walking down long hallways and climbing great staircases. Everywhere he tread, empty furniture and deserted rooms greeted him. His footsteps echoed loudly in the barren estate.

Where is everybody?

He called out, bidding anybody to appear, but his voice was answered by silence. As he walked, no longer taking heed of where his feet carried him, Brennan recalled the first memory he had of living in the house.

"One, two, three…" Maddy counted, covering her eyes with both hands. She paused and peeked out at Brennan. "You're supposed to go and hide now, dumdum."

He nodded sharply, and she began her count anew—at ten. He had ninety seconds to find a hiding spot, and he knew exactly where he would go.

Brennan took off at a dash, his footsteps silenced by the thick socks he wore. He climbed two flights of stairs and turned corners blindly as he distanced himself from her, his body invigorated with the energy only extreme youth could provide. He arrived in front of the room he had found the day before, an enormous room with empty shelves lining all four walls. Mom and Dad had yet to order new furniture, and there were only a few of the previous owners' pieces remaining, all covered in large, white tarps. He flung himself beneath one of them, rested on a chair, and quieted the excited giggle that rose to his lips.

"Ready or not, here I come!"

Brennan found himself standing in that same library now; his steps had led him here without thinking. He smiled slightly as he looked around the room. The shelves, solid units set inside alcoves in the wall, were less imposing than he had thought as a child; the tallest one was still within arm's reach for a man of Brennan's height. But the ambience had remained unchanged. The twilight of the setting sun filled the room, and motes of dust floated in and out of sight as they passed through the sunbeams. Brennan breathed deeply; the library had a delicious aroma to it, the smell of books and wood. He sat down heavily in one of the luxurious leather armchairs and let his fatigue flow out of him, down through the chair's pegs and into the aged hardwood floor. The room took away his pain and worries and it left him feeling relaxed, refreshed, and rejuvenated. He closed his eyes and let himself sink into the chair's comfortable embrace.

There was nothing in the world except his calm, steady breathing of the rich aroma of books. He felt a sense of ease and comfort that had been estranged from him for many years. The soft, golden light of the room was like a warm blanket over his weary eyes. In a way, this solitude was Brennan's personal form of paradise. He didn't believe in an afterlife, neither heaven nor hell; but this, here, this library and the life of leisure, this was his dream.

He had had it once, long ago.

"And it could be like this once again," said a soft voice. "Forever."

Brennan's eyes shot open. To his left, in the doorway, stood a slim figure of average height and reddish skin. It was the same man who had been impersonating a nurse in his nightmare. This time, he was dressed in the attire of a butler from Brennan's youth, complete with the Brennan family crest embroidered on the blazer.

"You have a beautiful home," the man commented, stepping lightly into the room.

Brennan watched him through veiled eyes. "You tried to kill me last time," he said. He shifted slightly in his seat, positioning for a better view of the would-be assassin.

The butler shrugged. "Those were my orders. Why would you leave such a life?" he asked, gesturing to the mansion in general.

"You're already inside my head," Brennan replied. "Why don't you find out for yourself?"

"I have tried," he said simply. "Your defenses are—" The butler hesitated. "You aren't the man I was expecting."

Brennan, sitting as he was in the comfortable

chair, barked out a harsh laugh. "That would be an understatement, to say the least. Were you even told *why* I was assigned as your target?" He chuckled in spite of himself. "I mean, come on, assassination on the first meeting?"

The butler stared at him silently, but his eyes spoke volumes.

"That's not what we do," Brennan continued. His voice was quiet, but it carried across the room like a deadly curse.

"I don't question orders," the butler said. There was an accusatory tone in his voice.

"And I don't follow them *blindly*. That's what can get a man killed."

"You know that we Sleepers can never retire, not with what we know."

"I'm out," Brennan said. "I'm living a normal life; just leave me be."

"Not with what we know," the butler repeated. "You're a threat, whether you realize it or not. With the knowledge you have, you can't be allowed to wander around unprotected and unsupervised. I'm here for your memory in service, nothing else."

"My memory…" Brennan said uncertainly.

"As a Sleeper, yes," the man replied, his voice measured and reasonable. "Nothing else."

Brennan was surprised, but the only reaction he

showed was narrowing his eyes by a hair. The powers of a Sleeper were incredible enough on their own. As far as Brennan knew, though, there was no such ability as memory-stealing in the repertoire of a Sleeper. If such a thing were possible, their dispute could end right here. But it would mean sacrificing his memories as a Sleeper, years of his life given to service. Years of obedience, betrayed by the actions of his former mentor.

And above all, Brennan didn't think it wise to let the Sleeper take another step closer.

"My memories are *mine*," Brennan growled. He sensed the other man tense in response, and he tried a different approach. "There was a reason I left the service. If I could just talk to you for a moment, man to man, you might realize you're playing for the wrong team."

The two men stared at each other from across the room.

"Those aren't my orders," the butler said softly.

The temperature of the room dropped suddenly. Wood groaned and creaked and splintered as the water trapped inside froze and expanded rapidly. The air became thick, like mud, and time slowed as the butler Sleeper went to draw a concealed knife from behind his back. From years of experience, Brennan knew that the Sleeper would turn the draw into a fluid throwing motion.

But he was prepared this time.

The moment that he had stepped into the library, he'd known that it was a trap. As wonderful as that room had been for him in his youth, the light had never been *that* beautiful nor had the books ever been *that* ornately arranged. The memory had been altered, romanticized, to make him want to stay and be calm and relaxed.

In a word, it was too *perfect*. And if Brennan knew anything by now, it was that the world wasn't perfect.

"This is my dream, dammit," he said, rising from the chair. His movement was fluid, prepared—and as fast as a striking cobra. He wrested control of the atmosphere away from the Sleeper and kept the slowing, numbing influence from touching him. Brennan crossed the room in two short strides and knocked the Sleeper off his feet with a powerful strike to the chest.

Upon later reflection, the fight was horribly one-sided.

The Sleeper arched gracefully as he glided slowly through the air from the punch. Brennan grabbed the man by the ankle and lashed him bodily in the opposite direction. He heard a pop as the Sleeper's ankle dislocated, and bones crunched when his face collided with the hardwood floor. The wooden boards, already weakened from the abrupt drop in temperature, cracked violently under the impact, and splinters of wood buried themselves in the man's face. His mouth gaped in a voiceless scream of agony.

Brennan approached the nearest block of bookshelves. With groans of protest, he gouged handholds in the wood with his bare hands. He ignored the blood that flowed in rivulets down his fingers. The wood shattered beneath his grip as he took hold of one side. He heaved mightily, his arms popping under the strain and the muscles of his back flexing painfully. Slowly, the bookshelf tipped forward from its alcove.

It moved slowly at first, like a tentative snowball rolling down a hill. As Brennan pulled it further and further toward its tipping point, it gained momentum, until it became an unstoppable avalanche. Books flew from the shelves like canaries from a mine, and then with a rush of air the entire structure fell upon the slowly writhing Sleeper with a terrible, sickening crash.

The pressure of the room abruptly vanished. Brennan's breath was visible in the cold room, but as he pulled back his mental efforts he no longer felt the Sleeper's numbing aura. He stood there, panting, bleeding. He could hear his pulse beating heavily in his ears; he twitched his hands as they regained feeling, and instantly regretted it. Shards of wood up to an inch long pierced his palms and fingers.

Brennan stood there and contemplated the fallen bookshelf for what seemed like a long time. The room around him never changed; the sun stayed perfectly poised in its position in the sky, and motes of dust swirled in the air without any regard for what had transpired. The other bookshelves, likewise, were neither impressed nor worried about their own future. His image of a perfect evening remained untouched by the Sleeper's passing.

The illusion wasn't of the Sleeper's making, said a small voice inside. Brennan ignored it. There was no perfect future in this house. Not anymore, not for him. He made his own way.

He left the library and walked down yet another hall. He was becoming more aware of the very real fatigue his body had felt before falling asleep, yet despite being aware of the dream, he was unable to wake up from it. He took it as a sign. The house was identical to that of his youth, and there had only been one adult-sized bed in the mansion at that time. He trusted his feet to carry him by memory to the master bedroom.

It was a large room, even for two people, and it was clean and orderly in the fashion following a visit from the maids. The bed was wide and long—perfect for Brennan—and he threw himself upon the soft covers. He laid his head to rest upon a platoon of pillows and let his eyes shut of their own accord.

It was his first peaceful sleep in a very long time.

φ φ φ

BRENNAN'S EYES FLUTTERED open and he rubbed the sleep from his face.

He cast a glance at the clock by his bed and had to do a double-take. It was afternoon already, and he had slept soundly for nearly seven hours. He felt a pang of guilt. Of course, he hadn't slept soundly. His mind dredged up the events of his dream, from the empty mansion of his youth to his brutal attack on the Sleeper. He hadn't killed the man—not physically— but he may as well have. The Sleeper would very likely be Fractured, lying near comatose in a room somewhere in the city. Brennan's stomach twisted with the thought.

A noise from the other room made him sit up in bed.

He prepared himself for the corresponding pain, but his body felt better. It felt great, in fact. There were still bruises on his ribs, but the aches and pains of the past twelve hours had melted away into merely uncomfortable reminders that made themselves known if he stretched the wrong way. He tested his shoulders, rolling them forward and back, and turned his head alternating in each direction until the stiffness in his neck cracked and popped away.

Another noise, and Brennan remembered that Bishop had taken the couch. Suddenly conscious of his nakedness, he slipped on a fresh pair of pants and checked himself in the mirror. He buttoned up a collared shirt as he left his bedroom.

On the couch, covered by a large gray blanket, was Bishop. Her head lay against one of the armrests, and gold hair fell across her sleeping visage. The blanket had been made for someone Brennan's size, and it wrapped around her small form twice. Very tightly around her form. Brennan's eyes drifted to the closet, inside of which were his washer and dryer. He could hear the telltale sound of clothes tumbling in the dryer, and he realized Bishop was completely naked beneath the blanket.

He gulped and moved quickly to the kitchen, grabbing a tall glass from the highest cupboard. From the fridge he grabbed orange juice and eggs, and he popped a slice of bread into the toaster as he heated up a skillet on the stove. By the time Bishop woke, he had breakfast sizzling and the dryer had finished its final spin.

"Brennan?" she asked sleepily. She rose slowly, keeping the blanket held against her. Sleeping against the armrest of the couch had given interesting temporary lines to her face. "Sorry, I must have dozed off longer than I…" Her voice trailed off. "Are you making breakfast?"

"It's the most important meal of the day."

Bishop inhaled sharply. "I am *starving*. Brennan, I could kiss you."

He wrinkled his nose and grinned. "Best not. You probably have morning breath right now."

"Alternatively, I could kill you," she suggested.

"Your clothes are ready," he told her, his grin growing wider.

Bishop wrapped the gray blanket more tightly around herself and marched over to the closet, liberating her warm, dry clothes and cradling them in a bundle under one arm. She paused at the entrance of the bathroom and looked back at him. "You look…healthy."

"I think that was almost a compliment."

She shook her head and laughed lightly. "Sorry, that came out poorly. But seriously, you look ten times better than yesterday."

Brennan lifted both arms and clasped his hands high over his head. His knuckles brushed against the ceiling. "Fit as a fiddle," he said. Truthfully, his shoulders were still sore and the movement was a bit stiff, but there was something about a full night's sleep that rejuvenated his spirit. Even though his body wasn't fully recovered, he *felt* better. "In fact, I need to call Sam right away."

Bishop grimaced, but she said nothing. She knew the score; McCarthy was part of the case, as aggravating to her as he might be. The bathroom door closed behind her as Brennan pulled the phone from his pocket. McCarthy picked up on the third ring.

"Brennan, what's up?"

"I need you to look into something, Sam."

"I don't know," McCarthy said. "I'm still waiting on this weekend's payment. Two days' work, cash."

"Yeah, yeah, I know the drill."

"And I'm still on retainer for Noel."

"Well I'm using her time, then. She's here with me now."

"Really? I'm near the station right now, I'll meet you—"

"No," Brennan said, cutting him off. "We aren't at the station, we're at my place."

There was a pause before Sam spoke again. "Arty, you sly dog," he said. Brennan could hear the grin in his voice. "I didn't know I had you to compete with as well."

"It's not like that," he sighed. He glanced uncertainly toward the bathroom, even though he knew Bishop couldn't overhear the call. "And I wouldn't get too hopeful on that front, if I were you.

Look, I'm taking Bishop back to her place now, so I won't be able to meet you at the station for another half hour. I need you to look into something while I'm away."

"What do you need?" Sam asked, sobering up instantly.

"We found out that the hallucinogen used in the patches is a drug called Chamalla."

"Chamalla? Huh, they must be a fan."

"A fan?"

"*Battlestar Galactica*?" Sam spoke slowly. His voice rang with disbelief. "Only the best sci-fi show to come out of the early 2000s."

"Huh. I didn't take you for a nerd, Sam."

"I believe the proper term is 'geek'." There was a brief pause. "And no, hey! That's not me!"

"Uh-huh, sure. Anyway, I need you to look into everywhere that Leviathan could be gaining access to it in large quantities. Hospitals, factories, anywhere."

"Leviathan, huh? Never heard of them."

"New outfit on the scene, I guess. If we move fast enough, we can shut them down here and now. My guess is we only have another day or two before they find another source of NicoClean patches, and if that happens, we'll have to start over from square one."

"Right." Brennan could hear a pen scribbling on paper on the other end. "I'll start looking and get back to you when I have something."

"Thanks, Sam."

Brennan ended the call, and Bishop emerged from the bathroom fully dressed in her dry clothes. Her face was bright and alert, though she still frowned at the phone in his hand. He wondered how Sam thought he had even the slightest chance of getting back into her good graces. Brennan doubted that she would ever open up to Sam like that again.

"What's so funny?"

Brennan didn't realize he had been smiling. "Just a bad joke that came to mind."

"Want to tell me what it was?"

"Maybe another time," he murmured.

The two of them dug into the breakfast Brennan had prepared, eating in companionable silence and letting the warmth of the food fill their bellies. When metal scraped against porcelain, Brennan collected the plates and rinsed them under the faucet, leaving them in a pool of sudsy water to be washed later.

He got the door for her, and they walked out into the hall. A minute later, they reached the bottom of the stairs and stepped out onto the street. The rain had stopped falling, and sunlight peeked through the clouds. His pocket vibrated just as they started walking toward the precinct. "One second," he said to Bishop. He lifted the phone to his ear. "Greg? What's going on? How is your mother?"

"Bad," his nephew replied. His voice shook speaking just that one word. "Uncle Arty, you need to come see her."

A heavy pit formed in Brennan's stomach. When Greg had called him the other day, he had sounded worried but still somewhat in control. Now, he seemed on the verge of hysterics, and Brennan found something incredibly unnerving in the way his nephew had chosen his words. *Come see her.*

"All right," he said, forcing his voice to remain calm. "Try to soothe her, keep her in bed, and I'll be right there."

"We aren't at home!" Greg said in a panicky voice.

"Where are you?"

"Come to the hospital."

CHAPTER EIGHTEEN

THE LIVING ROOM of the Scott ranch was a mess.

Before the storm abated in the valley, Nathaniel and Uncle Rick had taken over the living room, laying out a strategy for surveying the southern reach of the valley for future development. Their plan was to get to the Tower, assess the surviving infrastructure, and then see what could be done with the surrounding land. On the floor around the two men was a smattering of essential hiking supplies: boots, jackets, a compass and topographical map, several bottles of water, and some dried food.

Jeremy walked into the room just as his father shrugged on a waterproof jacket. "I want to come with you," he said.

"Absolutely not!" The three men turned toward the bedroom from which Annabelle's voice emanated.

Nathaniel frowned. "I have to agree with your mom on this one," he said. "We're going into some wild territory, and there's no telling what we might find there. Besides, the ground is slippery and unstable, and the storm could return at any minute."

"But you only need to look at the sky to see if it'll rain!" Jeremy argued. He leaned to peer out a window. "Oh, looks clear to me! And as for not knowing what is out there, that's exactly why I want to go! There could be more to the Tower, and I'm the only one who's been there for more than five seconds."

"Again with your tower," his father grumbled, swiping a hand across his chin.

"Well, hold on now," Uncle Rick chimed in, his voice placating. "Jeremy's right, we can see a storm coming from a good way off out here. And he is hardly a child anymore."

"Yeah, I'm not a kid," Jeremy agreed. But even he thought his voice sounded petulant. He puffed up his chest a bit under his father's scrutiny.

"All right," his father said finally.

Jeremy stared at him, his mouth slightly agape. "All right?"

"Yes," Nathaniel said. He shared a glance with Uncle Rick. "You can come with us."

"What?!" Annabelle sounded livid. She stormed into the living room and stood toe-to-toe with

Nathaniel. The air around her felt charged with anger.

Jeremy took a small step back from the meltdown about to happen.

"When did it become acceptable to make choices like this *without me*?" Her voice dripped with malice. "This is our son we're talking about! The last time he went off unsupervised, he nearly died!"

"He won't be unsupervised," his father challenged. "He'll be with me the whole time."

"*He* is standing right here," Jeremy piped in. Out of the corner of his eye, he saw Uncle Rick shake his head. Jeremy's eyes found the floor, chagrined, and he stayed out of the argument.

Annabelle scoffed. "Oh, yeah, big man in the office. Always the man with the plan. Tell me, what do *you* know about surviving in the wild? What happens if a mountain lion attacks, or if you get stuck in quicksand, or if *anything* happens?"

"Surviving in the wild? What do you think this is, a Robinson Crusoe survival story? We're basically camping in our own back yard, not wrestling crocodiles in the Amazon. We will be gone for a day, two days at the most."

"And I will be with them the entire time," Uncle Rick said, his deep voice sounding calm and reasonable.

His mother's glare danced between Nathaniel and

Uncle Rick. "If anything happens to my son—"

"Everything will be fine," Uncle Rick assured her, his eyes staying locked with hers.

The expression on Annabelle's face softened with those words, and she looked gratefully at him. "Keep them safe, won't you?"

Uncle Rick nodded. "I promise. You can count on me."

Placated, his mother hugged Uncle Rick briefly and turned to head to her room. She stopped at the threshold, though, and looked back at his father.

"This isn't over. And when you get back, we need to talk."

Nathaniel stood there, unmoving. "When we get back," he said. Annabelle nodded and entered her room, closing the door behind her. Jeremy looked at his father's back as their conversation echoed in his head.

Divorce.

He knew it the instant the thought came to mind. He had both sets of memories, and he knew the most recent years had been rough on their relationship. His mother had felt neglected as his father spent more and more time at work, away from her and the children. She had suspicions of secret lovers, or a mistress secretary, but Jeremy knew they were unfounded ideas.

His father, on the other hand, felt a constant

compulsion to provide for his family. That meant long hours in the office, deals that kept him working even on holidays, and family vacations cut short at the ring of the phone. It wasn't that Nathaniel was unaware of his wife's growing discontent. He had simply never been able to change.

Jeremy's thoughts leaped in an entirely different direction, and his mouth was moving before he could stop it. "I don't think mountain lions even live around here," he blurted out.

Uncle Rick smirked in amusement. "What train of thought took you there?"

"It just kind of jumps around sometimes," Jeremy said, feeling a burning sensation in his cheeks. "Do you think we could actually run into them? Mountain lions?"

"They're territorial and less likely to migrate than most, but those territories are huge, and they like to roam."

"When in Rome," Jeremy said. Uncle Rick cocked his head, and Nathaniel raised an eyebrow. "Well, because you have a big territory," he explained to his father. "And because we're about to…roam. When in roam."

Uncle Rick erupted with laughter, a deep bass rumbling that filled the room. Nathaniel cracked a smile. A light chuckle could even be heard coming from his mother's bedroom.

"That"—Uncle Rick wiped a tear from one eye—"was terrible."

There wasn't much time for talk after that as the men were swept up in a flurry of action. Nathaniel had purchased hiking supplies years ago, and the boots that Jeremy had received at that time were long since outgrown. He put on an old pair of his father's boots—which were a hair too large for his feet to fit in them comfortably—and shrugged into an oversized jacket. The sleeves hung down almost to his knuckles.

They set off later in the afternoon than Uncle Rick would have liked—he loudly voiced his opinion on the matter—and kept the rapidly falling sun to their right. In addition to their other supplies, Uncle Rick brought along a hunting knife, and Nathaniel now carried a deluxe, family-sized tent. "Now it's really like a camping trip," he had joked while packing. By the time they reached the one-mile point, Nathaniel was breathing heavily and straining from the weight on his back.

Likewise, blisters quickly emerged on Jeremy's feet. He was used to walking, both in the valley and around Odols, but the ill-fitting shoes chafed uncomfortably at the heels and sides of his feet. Still, he was thankful for them; they kept out the damp that seeped up from the ground with each soggy step.

The earth was completely saturated from the storm. What had before been rolling hills were now slippery mounds of mud which easily gave way underfoot, and the flat grasslands had been transformed into half-inch-deep marshes. The air never quite warmed up to the temperature it had been the day before, and now the sunlight was beginning to wane on them. If they didn't get dry soon, even the summer night air could settle a chill in them.

"I see it," Uncle Rick called finally. The sun was touching the slopes of the western mountains, and the trio had fallen into unequal paces during the hike. His uncle was at the top of a rocky outcropping, one which Jeremy knew had a good view of the Tower. Jeremy quickly joined him, jumping agilely from rock to rock until he reached the top. His pack was light, carrying only a few bottles of water, dried fruit, and the map. His father was less fortunate. The tent weighed heavily on him, and the five miles they covered before nightfall wore him down considerably. As formidable as he was in business meetings, he simply wasn't a man of great physical strength.

Up ahead was the old fort and the Tower at its center. The walls still looked as imposing to Jeremy as they had several days ago. It took another fifteen minutes or so for them to walk the distance between the rocky outcropping and the square entrance of the fort.

"My god, would you look at that?" Uncle Rick marveled, eyeing the stonework and the rusted portcullis still nestled in its recessed alcove above.

Nathaniel walked toward one of the outlying buildings and pushed hard against one of its wooden beams.

"Careful with that," Jeremy warned. "Some of these buildings are pretty rickety."

"And just how would you know that?"

"Um…they look old?" Jeremy felt his father's stare intensify. "And one sort of, kind of fell on me."

Nathaniel grunted. "So, naturally, your first impulse after that was to go *further* into the dangerous ruins."

Thankfully, Uncle Rick stepped between them with raised hands. "Enough of this." He placed one palm flat against the building and leaned. "I'm willing to bet this'll hold up. But we've got the tent anyway, and it doesn't look like rain tonight. Let's not chance it."

They eventually chose a spot in a corner of the fort; Uncle Rick reasoned that nothing would fall on them, but they'd still have walls on two sides to help the tent keep out the wind. The three of them worked in unison to assemble the tent, and Jeremy was astonished at the size of the thing. It could have easily

housed a group twice their size—with room to spare—
and the material was insulated without making the
inside sticky and cloying. It was top-of-the-line and had
never been used. They put the last piece in place just as
the shadows were reaching their full length, and Jeremy
knew the entire valley would soon be dark.

"Let's see the map," Nathaniel said. Jeremy
retrieved it from his backpack and Uncle Rick laid it
out in front of them. It was a large, rectangular sheet
of heavy paper, and it was completely blank.

"Nate, I thought you brought a—"

"You have to turn it on," he sighed. He placed a
thumb against one corner and swiped downward. The
paper burst into life as light and shadow danced across
its surface. Small beads embedded in the paper shifted
and molded themselves, and in an instant there was a
topographical map of Odols and its surrounding areas.
Nathaniel double-tapped the valley, and the beads
rearranged themselves. The edge of the paper lined
itself with miniature ink-black mountains in an almost-
complete circle, and the rises and dips of the valley
came into relief.

"Cool," Jeremy said, his fingers grazing along the
ridges of the mountains.

Uncle Rick huffed. "A simple map of ink and
paper would have sufficed."

"When you're a millionaire, then we can discuss

how you spend *your* money." Nathaniel pointed at a spot on the map. "We walked a good distance today, so we can probably survey as far as here tomorr—"

"I disagree," Uncle Rick interrupted. "Today, we were walking in a straight line, and it still took hours to walk five miles. Turn that into a circle, even with three people, we probably can't check out much further than this in one day." He moved Nathaniel's finger a few inches to the side, nearly halving the radius of their surveying circle. Just then, the map disappeared, its power flickering out.

"Right," Nathaniel coughed. "Umm, I never really opened the map after buying it. I assumed the charge would hold."

Uncle Rick sighed. "Never fail with paper and ink," he muttered.

"So what are we looking for?" Jeremy asked.

"Before we can start building anything, we need to know *what* to build and *where* to build it," Uncle Rick said. "This valley is breathtaking, so I'm thinking maybe a resort for all seasons. Sledding in the winter, camping in the summer, with a beautiful landscape all year 'round."

"Okay," Jeremy said. "So we're looking for somewhere with a nice view, basically?"

"Precisely," Nathaniel said, clasping Jeremy's shoulder.

Uncle Rick rubbed at his chin. "Before we left the outcropping, I saw what looked like a large lake glimmering a few miles to the west. We could reach it by midday if we set out early tomorrow, and then we won't be squandering our efforts on a small circle around this fort."

Nathaniel groaned. "My back is killing me," he said. "And these boots really cut into your feet."

"We could leave the tent here," Jeremy suggested. "Keep it set up for tomorrow night. That way we don't have to break it down in the morning, and we have a place ready for us after we go see the lake."

"And I won't have to carry the damned thing on my back," his father added.

Uncle Rick frowned at the two of them, clearly uncomfortable with the idea, but he agreed. "Get some sleep," he told them. "It's going to be a long day tomorrow."

ф ф ф

JEREMY KNEW INSTANTLY that he wasn't dreaming, nor was he drawing on any of his stolen memories.

Once again, he was standing in the Jardin des Anges. It was a strange night, though; there was a chill in the air, and the temperature dropped even more in the minutes that followed. Plants withered before his eyes, their leaves crumpling inward in a desperate attempt to escape the oncoming freeze.

"Hello, Jeremy," said an old, kind, and familiar voice. It was Benjamin. The man made himself visible as he stepped out from behind a hardy shrub with prickly leaves. "It is good to see you again."

"I'm supposed to be sleeping…is it still considered rest if we're doing, well, this?" Jeremy asked. He glanced around the garden, but it seemed that they were alone. "What am I doing here?"

"I brought you here."

"You can do that?"

Old Ben smiled. "There are many things of which you are not yet aware. This is but one skill you will learn…in time. For today, we will start small."

"Today?"

The plants fell away into the ground, suddenly being replaced by solid brick walls and a large plot of sand, dotted here and there by wide rocks. Old Ben took a few steps forward and looked at the room appraisingly, apparently unhindered by his lack of sight. "A Zen garden…hmm. Not what I would have expected."

"Wh-what is this place?" Jeremy asked.

"You do not recognize your own mind? This is most unfortunate." Benjamin sat directly on the sand with his legs crossed under him. "No time like the present, as they say. Jeremy, tell me everything you know about Sleepers."

"I don't understand…"

"I *do* have all night, but I would rather that we moved along quickly," the old man said somewhat shortly. "Tell me what you already know about Sleepers."

Jeremy sat as well and scratched his nose as he thought. "You…enter people's dreams and make them go crazy?"

Old Ben gave no reaction. "Go on."

"You're kind of on the same level as Bigfoot and Nessie, in terms of actually existing. Now I know better, but a few days ago, I was in the same camp as everyone else. I didn't think Sleepers were real."

"Hmm." He sounded disappointed. "And what do you suppose this place represents?"

"My…mind?"

"Yes and no. This is your Sleeperscape. Every Sleeper has a dwelling such as this somewhere in their minds. It is a place of retreat, of safety, and also the source of our legendary power."

"I don't understand."

Old Ben gestured to a nearby rock. "This boulder represents the mind of someone in Odols, and particularly one whom you have met." He glanced at the brick walls and grimaced. "But you have lived a sheltered life, one with barriers that prevent you from experiencing much of what this world has to offer. Thus, your Sleeperscape is small and secluded. You have few nodes through which to access others' minds."

All of this information was almost too much for Jeremy, but his brain raced to keep up. "What happens if I touch one of the rocks?" he asked hesitantly.

Benjamin's lips spread in a crinkly smile. "Finally, a question worth asking, and deserving of an answer. Why not find out for yourself?"

Jeremy stared at the nearest rock. It was smaller than a lot of the others in the room, with smooth, rounded edges. He reached out to it across the sand, but his hand hesitated just above the surface. "It won't hurt, will it?"

Benjamin solemnly shook his head.

And Jeremy touched the rock.

His brain was flooded with a swirling torrent of images before he found himself sitting in an almost familiar place. Soft dirt and sand molded between his fingers as he pressed his hand against the ground. Placid, black water filled a shallow pool surrounded by soaring black walnuts. Chirping laughter drew Jeremy's attention to the side.

Ellie came running in from the forest. Two large, red-furred squirrels followed closely on her heels. She giggled as one of them leapt onto her pant leg and scurried its way up onto her shoulder, and they fell in a heap just a few yards away from Jeremy. She didn't seem to have noticed him.

This must be what Ellie dreams about, Jeremy realized.

She stood and raised a hand high over her head, and the squirrels abruptly fell still and watched her with small, beady eyes.

Jeremy wasn't quite sure what he was seeing. He'd witnessed Ellie interacting with the valley animals before, but never like this. When had she had time to tame them to that extent? He knew this was only a dream, but it was so starkly reminiscent of her daytime behavior that he wondered how much of it was based in reality.

"Wow, that's awesome," Jeremy murmured.

Ellie whipped around and stared intensely at where he sat. Her eyes scrunched a bit at the corners. "Jeremy? Is that you?"

He waved, and her eyes lightened. "Hey, Ellie."

"What are you doing here?"

"I just…" His voice trailed off. How would he explain his presence in her dream? "Uh, Mom sent me to bring you in for dinner."

"Oh." She looked down at the squirrels, but they'd scattered back into the trees. Her face fell when she saw the empty patch of grass. "I guess I'll get headed back…" She turned back to Jeremy. "But how did you find—?"

A curtain of black fell over the landscape, and Jeremy was knocked back into his sand garden. Benjamin sat absolutely still, not having moved an inch.

"It all just went away!" Jeremy said. "How do I get back in?" He placed his hand against the rock, but it was cold and unyielding.

"They are awake, I imagine," Old Ben said. "May I ask whose mind you entered?"

"It was my sister."

"Intriguing. And what did you learn?"

Jeremy laughed. "That I'm not very good at being a Sleeper. She woke up almost immediately after I arrived."

A bemused smirk crossed Old Ben's lips. "Subtle immersion is a learned skill. Given time, your talents will improve. I once had a student who took *years* to become proficient in the art of seeing without being seen, being present without being noticeable. That you were able to enter the dream at all is a tremendous feat, though. Your future holds promise."

Pride swelled in his chest, and Jeremy grinned like an idiot. "Thank you."

Old Ben nodded. "Now, get some sleep." Suddenly, the room was empty, but his voice lingered even as his body faded from view. "Until we meet again."

CHAPTER NINETEEN

MADDY WAS ON her death bed.

Brennan had arrived at the hospital in the early afternoon, but he could do little but wait helplessly as the doctors and nurses worked to stabilize his sister. He and Greg sat in stony silence as the night wore on. His nephew seemed strung out, worse than he had looked the last time they'd met, and Brennan knew he was going through Chamalla withdrawal. The timing couldn't have been worse for the young man; he would want to escape reality now more than ever.

Before the clock struck eight, a doctor emerged from the operating room. His gloves were coated with blood. He threw them in the trash before removing his surgical mask. Greg blanched at the sight of his mother's blood. He looked like he was going to be sick to his stomach. Brennan's heart felt for the young man.

He was struggling to cope with Maddy's sudden downturn, too.

It had seemed like just yesterday they were playing hide-and-seek.

"Doctor," he said, shaking hands with the man in white. "How is she?"

"She's stable, but still critical." He led Brennan away from Greg and spoke in a hushed whisper. "We had to drill holes to relieve some of the pressure in her skull. It has slowed the swelling, but—" The doctor hesitated, and Brennan felt his heart turn cold. "Your sister slipped into a coma shortly after surgery."

Icy tendrils spread throughout his body. His hairs raised on end, and he felt his mind go numb. The doctor said something that he couldn't hear, as if the words were drowned before they could reach him.

"What was that?" he asked. His voice betrayed him, and the doctor put a hand on his shoulder.

"I said that I would seriously recommend seeking professional help."

"You're a professional," Brennan said. "That's why we're here. Help her, please."

The doctor frowned and shook his head sadly. "Not help for her," he said. "A grief counselor, for him." He gestured with his eyes toward Greg, who was huddled on the floor with a vacant expression on his face.

It was a moment before the full impact of his words hit Brennan. "No," he said. "Not again. Maddy is my sister, she's all I have left!" His voice was a harsh whisper. His eyes, bloodshot and rimmed with tears, searched the doctor's desperately. He kept his words low so that Greg wouldn't overhear. "There must be something else you can try. Anything."

"I'm afraid there is little more that we can do," the doctor replied. He looked mournfully back at the operating room. "Even if this were a normal case, the chances of recovering from a coma diminish with each day that passes. In her condition, I'm not sure such a thing would even be possible."

In her condition. Brennan understood. Hell, he had even gone through it before. But knowledge and experience did nothing to soften the blow, to lessen the loss he felt. His sister was all he had left. And she was all Greg had *ever* had.

The mind was a fragile thing. Strong mental assaults could Fracture a mind, such as he had done to the Sleeper in the library. In Maddy's case, it was the result of an overzealous use of Chamalla's predecessor in the drug market. Her mind and body no longer connected properly. It was no great secret that Maddy's life had been shortened after being Fractured; in many ways, she was already dead.

"Damn you," Brennan growled. He didn't know

if he was cursing God, or the doctor, or even himself, but he knew that someone, somewhere, had hell to pay for this. He looked at Greg with the knowledge that his mother was on death's door. There was no coming back from that.

The doctor patted his arm lightly and gave them a moment. Brennan walked over and joined his nephew on the floor. Greg continued to stare at the wall, disconnected, obviously trying to keep his emotions from overwhelming him. Only the occasional sniffling of his nose gave him away. Brennan waited patiently, knowing that no amount of words could console him if he wasn't receptive to it. It was a while before Greg finally wiped a hand at his eyes and spoke.

"What did the doctor say?" he croaked.

Brennan chose his words carefully. "They operated on her," he said, "and they managed to relieve some of the swelling in her brain. She's stable now."

"Do they know what happened?"

"He didn't say. My guess is that her condition just got worse."

"It's treatable, though. She's better since the surgery, right?" he asked hopefully. "When can we go see her?"

Guilt banged relentlessly against Brennan's heart. Receiving the news—and accepting it—was the worst part of the grieving process. He had heard it years ago when Mara had been slipping away. His reaction had been less than stellar; in fact, he had tempted fate in his mad denial of the truth. Brennan wished he could be anywhere other than here, yet he knew this was exactly where he needed to be. With Greg, and with Maddy, until the end.

"Greg," he started, "I don't know any other way to say this but to give it to you straight. And I need you to listen to me when I say this, because it's the truth. Do you understand?"

His nephew nodded slowly, his lower lip trembling. Brennan steeled himself. It was one thing to receive the news, to go through that kind of anguish; it was another thing entirely to be the messenger.

"Maddy was a kind and loving sister to me, even when we were little kids growing up. She always looked after me, and she always had time to play games on my schedule. And as we grew up, we stayed close—though now I wish I could have spent more time with her. Perhaps I could have kept her on the straight and narrow…" He broke off and chuckled at the absurdity of that thought. "Though the straight and narrow was never a path that interested your mother."

Greg's eyes were glossy with unrealized tears, but he still managed a weak smile.

"Anyway," Brennan said with a sobering sniffle, "she soon became pregnant and had you. You could not have found a more glowing mother anywhere. She absolutely adored you, and you were the light of her life ever since that day. To hear her go on about you, your first steps, first words, first crush in school—it's what eventually convinced your Aunt Mara and I to try and start a family of our own. You were everything to her."

At those words, Greg broke down in unabashed sobs. Brennan pulled his nephew against him and let his shirt be darkened with tears as he cradled him under one arm. Not all of the tears were Greg's.

"It would be an injustice to say she didn't live a full life. She laughed, she lived, and she loved. There isn't anything left here for her to do," he said gently. "Now it's our turn to honor her life, her legacy, and let her move on."

Greg shook as he huddled against Brennan's massive frame. His sobs racked his whole body, and they rose in volume as he poured out his grief. It was a deep release of emotion, and Brennan knew that his nephew understood that his mother's body couldn't stay plugged into the machines any longer. Brennan grieved, but he found that most of his grief was transformed into sympathy for his nephew, who would not soon forget the pain he now felt.

"Greg," Brennan said after a long while. It was deep into the night when he spoke. "Do you want to say goodbye?"

His nephew looked up wordlessly and nodded.

They entered the hospital room where Maddy Warner was still hooked up to a machine. It was a dark room, empty of anyone but the three of them. Greg went and took his mother's hands between his own. Brennan watched fresh tears roll down his nephew's cheeks as he spoke quietly, his last words to her a secret soliloquy. Some time passed, and the boy finally let go of her hands. She was a pale and silent statue, and Brennan took a moment to remember her as she had been, a smiling little girl playing with her brother.

A single tear escaped and slipped down along Brennan's jaw as Greg returned to him by the door. He said one final farewell to his sister, and uncle and nephew alike were reluctant to leave the room. Finally, they departed in silence, leaving Maddy's spirit to find its way.

CHAPTER TWENTY

THE MORNING SUN was a welcome relief in the valley.

Warm light dried the caked mud of their footprints and helped turn much of the marshes back into grasslands. Unfortunately for Jeremy and his father, Uncle Rick insisted on starting their trek two hours before sunrise, and today's hike hardly fared better than yesterday's.

Still, the chill in the air following the storm had dissipated, and the skies were clear for as far as the eye could see. It seemed that fortune was finally favoring them. They made good progress without having to break camp and carry the tent, and the journey to the lake that Uncle Rick had spotted was an easy one. They passed through open fields broken here and there by small forest glades. The grasses grew as high as Jeremy's waist, and he heard small creatures scurrying about in the underbrush near his feet. This was an untamed wilderness that was unaccustomed to humans; they had never learned to fear them. Maybe that was how Ellie had gained such easy control over them, both in reality and in her dreams.

They crested one final hill before the lake was in sight. It reflected the morning sun and stretched for at least a mile before them. A forest of tall pines surrounded the lake, and its shimmering surface was spotted with a smattering of tiny islands. A flock of birds flew over the water as the three men looked on from the hilltop.

"It's beautiful," Jeremy said in awe.

"That it is," Nathaniel agreed. "I bet we'll be getting visits all year 'round just to see a view like this." The lake glittered like a diamond under the rising sun.

Uncle Rick cupped his hands into fleshy binoculars and peered about. "There," he said, pointing to an adjacent hill. "That's where we should build. It'll have a perfect view of the lake during the day and still be able to see the sunset from indoors. Imagine a seasonal hotel with swimming in the summer and ice skating in the winter."

Nathaniel nodded. "We should go check it out, though, and make sure that it's solid enough for building."

Uncle Rick nodded. "Get the lay of the land."

"Exactly."

Jeremy took off before his father had finished the word. He was getting hungry, and the sooner they arrived at the other hill, the sooner they could break for lunch.

He grievously misjudged the distance. It was a solid hour of hiking through tall grass and thick brambles, and the three men were sweating heavily by the end of it, even Uncle Rick. The heat of the summer sun was returning, and it didn't do them any favors.

"Let's stop here," his uncle suggested. Jeremy and Nathaniel both fell onto their knees without protest. Uncle Rick leaned against a boulder and took out a water bottle. "You two should be drinking, too," he said firmly. "You need to stay hydrated, or you'll collapse before you even realize there's a problem."

Jeremy nodded tiredly and retrieved a bottle each for himself and his father.

"Look at this view, Nate," his uncle continued. He breathed deeply, his barrel chest expanding to an impressive size. He clambered on top of the boulder and sighed in contentment. "This is definitely the spot. Smell that fresh air! When that lake freezes over in winter, you're going to have yourself a fantastic place for ice skating."

"Uncle Rick," Jeremy said, "can you finish your story from yesterday? The one where you were lost in

Brazil?"

He looked down at his nephew in surprise. "That's right, I never completed it, did I? All right, well, I've forgotten where I was in the story…"

"You were disguised as local militia," Jeremy supplied immediately. "And there was a drug lord."

Uncle Rick gazed at him with a peculiar look in his eye. "Yes, of course. You have the memory of an elephant," he praised.

You don't know the half of it, Jeremy thought. His father moved in closer to hear the story as well. Uncle Rick positioned himself so his feet dangled off the boulder and he cleared his throat.

"Right, well. My buddy Jimmy and I were deep in hostile territory now, *deep* in the shit. We couldn't drink a lick of the water; breathing the air was bad enough, humid as it was."

"Why couldn't you drink the water?" Jeremy asked.

"It was poisoned," his uncle said matter-of-factly. Nathaniel sat up a little straighter upon hearing that. "That was our mission, you see? We couldn't stop their drug smuggling; there were just too many shipments on the ground and coming by sea for that kind of approach. And if we dropped in and snuffed *el jefe*, the next man in line would just take charge."

"I think they speak Portuguese in Brazil," Jeremy

said.

"Would you stop interrupting?" His words were plaintive, but Uncle Rick's smile betrayed his natural amusement. "As I was saying, there was no stopping the shipments and no headhunting. So we poisoned the water supply. Hell of a drug, it was; knocks out the immune system in hours and carries pheromones at the same time. We lowered their ability to fight infection, then the pheromones attracted mosquitoes and other nasty things." He scratched at a phantom itch in his neck. "I think that's what attracted so many of the blighters to us, actually. We must've breathed in enough of the water vapor to make us attractive, but without the lowered immune response."

Nathaniel held up a hand. "Hang on," he said. "That was a lot of unfamiliar mumbo jumbo bio-talk coming from my big brother, the harmless world traveler. And since when did you start *killing* people?"

"They were bad guys, Dad," Jeremy said in his uncle's defense. He turned to look into Uncle Rick's face. "You only killed the drug lord and his cartel, right?"

"Of course! Nobody else got hurt," he reassured them.

"Well, that's a relief," Nathaniel said. He stood and stretched, and a few places in his spine popped in response. He took a long stride away toward a copse of trees. "Back in a minute. Nature calls."

"I'll alert the media," Uncle Rick yelled after him. He jumped down from the top of the boulder and landed heavily beside Jeremy, who could have sworn the ground quivered slightly.

"Woah, watch it there!" Jeremy cried, sidestepping his uncle's landing. The two of them leaned against the enormous rock and admired the beautiful vista. "Was that story true? Did all of that really happen?"

Uncle Rick chuckled and tugged his beard scruff absently. "Every word of it," he replied, his voice deep and rich and jolly again. "I really enjoyed my time down south, though, apart from the work. Nice people, great food."

Something still nagged at the edge of Jeremy's thoughts, and he had to concentrate to realize what it was. "Growing up, I always thought that you were a world traveler."

"I am! All seven continents, many times," he boasted.

Jeremy sighed. "No, I mean, as a *peaceful* traveler. Like, sightseeing, getting your picture in front of the Louvre and the Pyramids. Something more along the lines of Peace Corps, or the Foreign Legion."

"You have to be French to do that."

"The way you tell it, it sounds like you were a

mercenary."

"I prefer to think of myself as a sort of secret agent," he said, puffing out his chest.

"I don't think secret agents are supposed to announce that they're secret agents," Jeremy said with a laugh.

"I'm retired." Uncle Rick peered out into the distance. "What's that?"

Nathaniel came crashing through the trees, screaming incoherently. His pants were unfastened, and he held them up with one hand as he sprinted toward the two of them. He waved with his free arm as he shouted.

"Bear!" he yelled. "Run, move, NOW!"

Behind him, a roar rose up from within the trees.

Nathaniel tripped and fell as he secured his pants, and Uncle Rick moved to pick him up even as he pushed Jeremy forward with one arm. They moved with speed that only hysteria could inspire, the mania that pushed bodies past their breaking point and gave mothers the strength of ten bodybuilders. Jeremy had never pumped his legs so fast or so hard in his life, and he heard his heart pounding against his chest.

Running was awkward in his too-large boots, and more than once he threatened to twist an ankle on an unlucky step. It was only Uncle Rick's constant speed and strength that kept them moving, and they reached the hill from which they'd first spotted the lake in under twenty minutes. The last part of the run was an uphill climb, and Jeremy collapsed on the ground when they reached the top.

His father was in no better shape. He wheezed and clutched at his chest, which his sweat-soaked shirt was clinging to tightly. Uncle Rick breathed loudly beside him, winded but without any other obvious discomfort. Jeremy felt his aching feet covered in a thin film of fluid; most or all of his blisters must have broken during the sprint.

"Did you get a good look at it?" Uncle Rick finally asked.

Nathaniel shook his head. "It was…big. Really big." He looked him up and down for a moment. "Maybe even bigger than you."

"At least you have the energy to make jokes," Uncle Rick said grimly.

Nathaniel sobered quickly. "Right. It was enormous—"

"You've already said that."

"—and it had black fur all over."

"A black bear in these parts…during summer? Are you certain?" Uncle Rick earned a level look from his brother. "All right," he said, hands up. "Then the best thing for us to do—"

Another roar sounded, not too far away from

where they stood. They could hear something large scraping the bark from trees as it lumbered through the nearby forest. Uncle Rick squarely faced the two of them.

"You need to go. Now!"

"What about you?" Jeremy asked.

His uncle gripped him by the hand to hoist him up, and Jeremy's vision blurred and magnified at the same time.

It was a wholly unnerving experience, and it took Jeremy a moment to realize what had happened. In all their time together, he and his uncle had never made skin-to-skin contact. The firm grip was like a vise on his arm, one he couldn't escape. Memories flooded his waking mind without warning, sudden recollections of a past that wasn't his—only now it was. Experiences filled his brain to bursting, every recounted story from his childhood suddenly reinforced with visceral knowledge, the memory of every adventure. He was drowning in it.

"Jeremy, pick up those feet and run," came his uncle's urgent voice.

There was something else in there, too. It was engrained in his voice, burning with its own dancing fire of life. It was something deep and rich. Why hadn't he noticed that before?

"Take your father and go! Don't stop until you get

home!" commanded the fathomless voice.

Jeremy felt his legs moving without his brain telling them to. But it was a good idea, wasn't it? He was supposed to run. His clumsy steps lengthened into a loping run, and he felt his father's presence beside him. But that was the only presence. Jeremy glanced over his shoulder in alarm.

Behind them, armed with only a small knife, his uncle stayed to confront the bear.

CHAPTER TWENTY-ONE

BRENNAN'S APARTMENT ONCE more became a den for two.

He didn't think that leaving Greg alone last night would have been a good thing, so the two of them had returned to his apartment after leaving the hospital. He let his nephew take the bed while he slept on the couch, but Greg's soft sobs could be heard through the wall, and neither one of them got much rest until Greg finally cried himself to sleep. It was an exhausting thing, being miserable, and Brennan sympathized with the kid. He had made his peace with losing Maddy a long time ago; it was just hitting his nephew fresh that she was gone.

Brennan made the executive decision to stay home that day. The two of them needed a personal day, and he cracked open two bottles of Coke just as Greg emerged from the bedroom. He didn't say anything, and Brennan didn't want to overstep his bounds. It had occurred to him sometime in the early morning that Greg would need someone to watch over him. He was eighteen, but his age mattered little with no job and no aspirations for college. He was an addict, and Brennan was the only family he had left.

"Good morning," Brennan said, offering a Coke.

Greg turned it down. "It's afternoon," he replied. He sat on the couch, which protested with a whoosh of air as he sank into the cushion. "And that stuff rots your teeth, you know."

Brennan grunted. "More for me. Do you want to watch something?"

"Yeah, sure," Greg said. He picked up the remote and turned the television on, but didn't so much as glance at the screen. Brennan sighed and joined him on the couch, placing the second bottle of Coke on the end table.

His nephew looked at the floor. There were a few shards of glass that Brennan had missed in his hasty clean-up the night before. Greg raised an eyebrow. "Should I ask?"

"Best if you don't."

"That wasn't really an open question," he countered. "What happened?"

Brennan chewed at the inside of his mouth. Greg

was a good kid, and he was hurting for some kind of connection right now. Brennan had become accustomed to shutting away his thoughts and feelings, compartmentalizing everything, and he had never been the best at opening up to people. Now he had been asked to do it twice in less than twenty-four hours.

He had never been forthright about his past as a Sleeper; in fact, every Sleeper to date had served until death, and Brennan's situation was unique as far as he knew. Nobody had bothered with the details of *retirement*. Which, he supposed, meant that there were no restrictions against revealing his past. Still, Sleepers were feared by many, regardless of their status as fact or fiction. He wasn't sure how his nephew would react to the news.

"It's complicated," he hedged.

Greg looked at him and sighed. "Look, if you just went on a bender and lost it, I'm old enough to understand."

"What? No! It wasn't anything like that." Brennan wished it were so simple. He took a deep breath and turned to face his nephew. "Okay, what I'm about to tell you, you can't repeat to anyone. Understand? Absolutely nobody."

"Got it."

"I'm serious," he said gravely. "If anybody were to find out that—"

Greg met his eyes. "Uncle Arty, you can trust me."

True.

Brennan didn't need any further proof. He pursed his lips, choosing his words carefully. "A couple of nights ago, a Sleeper visited me in one of my dreams." Greg arched a skeptical eyebrow but said nothing. "I was dreaming about your Aunt Mara, she was—I was visiting her by her bedside. It wasn't a dream, really, so much as a memory. Every detail was exactly the same, right down to the doctor pronouncing her dead while her heart was still beating. I was just about to try the impossible when the Sleeper appeared. I didn't even notice him until it was almost too late."

"But it was just a dream, right? Sleepers aren't real, and even if—"

"No," Brennan said, cutting him off. "It's never just a dream, not when Sleepers are involved. They are very real, Greg." He hesitated, but remembered what his power had told him. Greg could be trusted. "I used to be one of them."

"You were…no. You're a cop, a detective."

"I am now," he said simply.

Greg gaped at him for a long moment, then reached over Brennan and grabbed the second Coke from the end table. He took a long drink from it, several swallows, before sitting back and staring into empty space. "Okay," he said finally.

"Okay?" Brennan looked at his nephew incredulously. "That's all?"

He shrugged. "It's in the past, right? Sleepers are the boogeymen and whatever, but that's not you." He looked at Brennan with mature eyes. "Now you're a cop."

They exchanged that stare for a moment, and it was Brennan who looked away first. His eyes burned with unfamiliar tears—not of sorrow, but of pride. His nephew was growing up.

"Thank you for understanding," Brennan said, his voice heavy. He took a long sip that finished his Coke, and he reached forward to put the empty bottle on the glass tabletop—the one that had been shattered. He checked the motion and instead replaced it on the end table.

"So you still didn't explain *that*," Greg said with a smile, gesturing to the empty space before them. A sliver of glass gleamed against the wood in the afternoon sun, and Brennan picked it up tenderly.

"I woke up," he said, grinning like a wolf. "I've always known the day would come when a Sleeper would appear in my dreams. I slept with a thumb tack curled in my palm, in case I ever needed to wake up in a pinch." He walked over to the kitchen and tossed the glass shard into the trash.

"Slept. Past tense," Greg noted. "You aren't still using it?"

Brennan shrugged. "The last time we met, it didn't end well for him. I figure I have some breathing room for the time being. As long as I keep quiet, they have no reason to come for me."

"Keep quiet about what?"

He looked at his nephew, and his tone was very solemn. "Sleepers *are* the boogeymen." His pocket vibrated then, and he took out his phone. "Sam," he said. "What've you got for me?"

"Arty, I have good news and bad news. Which would you like first?"

"Surprise me."

"Bad news is that there were a surprising number of places that either produce or store Chamalla, and it was a pain and a half tracking them all down. I'm charging double for all of this legwork."

Brennan remembered that Sam was still technically on retainer for Bishop. "Done," he promised. "What's the good news?"

"Being the trusty and thorough friend that I am, I found all of these places for you *and* managed to narrow down the list of likely suspects to two locations."

"Excellent!" Brennan said. "Sam, I could kiss you."

"Please don't."

"All right, what are the addresses?" He wrote them down as Sam read them to him.

"But there's a catch," Sam added. "These spots are across town from each other, too far apart for you to visit one and then the other."

Brennan followed his logic. "If Leviathan is watching both of them, they'd have enough of a warning to clear out if we don't hit the right one first."

"Exactly. So what are you going to do?"

"I'll call Bishop and organize strike teams on both locations. We'll converge simultaneously and mop them up before they have a chance to react."

"Sounds good, partner. Need anything else on my end?"

"No need," Brennan said. "Thanks for your help. I'll see to it that you get your money when this is all over." *I don't know how the hell I'm going to break that news to Bishop,* he thought, ending the call. He motioned for Greg to join him. "I'm taking you back to your place," he said. "Something came up at work, and I have to go."

"Can't I stay here?"

He hesitated. He rarely had guests over, except for Bishop yesterday and Sam's occasional visits. With Maddy's passing, would Greg have to live with him now? It was probably safer for him—mentally, at least—not to go back to his place just yet.

"I, um…sure," Brennan finally said. "Teeth-rotting fluid is in the fridge, and you know how to work the television. Just watch your feet. There could still be glass lying about."

Greg grinned. "I'll be careful, I promise."

Brennan smiled back, but then he noticed something. His nephew's eyes were sunken, and the skin around them was sallow. The rest of his face had a grayish tinge to it. He had chalked it up to poor sleep, or maybe he had just been too tired himself to recognize the symptoms, but now he saw that Greg was still suffering from Chamalla withdrawal.

He forced cheer into his smile and said his farewell, then descended the stairs to the street while dialing Bishop's number. She answered on the second ring.

"Brennan, how is Maddy?" He broke the news to her. "I'm so sorry," she said. "I know what it's like to lose somebody you love."

"It's never easy," he said. His voice was suddenly hoarse, and he forced the sudden surge of emotion away. It was time to work. "That isn't why I called, though."

"Oh? Did Sam find something?"

Brennan ignored the tone she used when saying Sam's name and told her what he had found out. "You and I will be leading the strike teams," he said. "I'm heading into the station now to round up everyone I can. There's no time for you to come here, so I'll send the team to rendezvous with you uptown."

"Understood," she said. Her voice turned mournful for a moment. "And Arthur? If you need someone to talk to—about Maddy, or anything—I'm here to listen."

His heart thudded heavily in his chest. "Thanks," he said, and then he hung up.

It took less than an hour to organize the uniforms they needed and divide them into two strike teams. One was sent uptown to assist Bishop while the other remained with Brennan to move in on a warehouse on the eastern fringe of the city. They took the shuttle and arrived just as the sun was starting to touch the skyline to the west. It was a large industrial park, full of different buildings ranging from old, square cinderblock monstrosities to newer, prefabricated modular units. An abandoned smelting workshop sat beside a dilapidated lumber mill, the kind that had cut and stored thousands of logs per day over a century ago. They were now silent relics in an industrial graveyard.

Brennan and his men took up positions outside of a long warehouse made of steel and stone. They all wore bulletproof vests and carried semiautomatic rifles slung over their shoulders. Despite all of the added weight, they moved like ghosts alongside the building. Brennan wore a simple band of black glass on his wrist. He tapped it twice, and an acknowledgement light winked twice in response. He just hoped that nothing gave away their position until he received the signal. A quiet breeze drifted through the air, stirring up dust around their feet and causing rusted metal to creak somewhere in the park.

This was the hardest part of any mission—the waiting. Being on guard and prepared for anything was fine for a few minutes at most, after which point the tedium could set in with little effort. Snipers were trained to maintain alertness for hours or days at a time, and Sleepers were similarly conditioned, but it was not something typical of uniformed police.

Lights flashed on his wrist, a single dot of light in a rapid three-burst pulse. That was the signal that Bishop was ready at her position uptown. Brennan sent a confirmation back and silently signaled his squad into action.

They entered in a burst of sound and light that brought the warehouse to life. Brennan slid open the sheet-metal door that separated his squad from the interior, and thick boots made heavy footfalls as they stormed the building. They flicked on the flashlights mounted to their rifles, and beams of light swept corners and catwalks as they entered. Empty wooden pallets lined the walls on either side, with only a few still bearing large, wooden crates. Steel beams crisscrossed overhead, the lights hanging from them having long since burned out. It was a large warehouse, but seemingly empty; their footsteps echoed off the cavernous walls.

No cries of protest rang out; no gunfire, no fanfare. Two men entered the back office and yelled, "Clear!" Similar shouts were called from the upper walkways. Whatever this place had been, it wasn't Leviathan's source of Chamalla. Brennan swore and swept a hand across his sweat-beaded brow.

"Sir," one of the officers called. "You'll want to take a look at this."

He moved to join the officer, who had his rifle trained on one of the crates. It was labeled 'FRAGILE' on the outside, and one of the sides had already been cracked open and left that way before they entered. There was a single square package laying inside, no thicker than a travel brochure. One solitary patch.

"Discarded NicoClean, sir," the officer said upon seeing what was inside. "Sorry, thought it was important." He moved to replace the missing side of the box.

"Hold on," Brennan said, moving to pick up the patch. He looked it over on the outside and didn't find any tear in the wrapping. It definitely wasn't the refuse of some random person quitting smoking. Tentatively, he ripped a small tear in the top of the wrapper and gently wafted the scent toward his nose. The hairs on his neck stood on end. He felt the room spin slightly beneath his feet, and he quickly sealed up the patch again. It was definitely saturated with Chamalla—a fully converted patch.

"They were here," he growled, his anger rising. He felt his pulse quicken and he ran his fingers through his hair. The reason behind leaving a single patch to be found was only too clear. "Damn it, they were here and now they're toying with us!"

Even as his emotions raged, some compartment of his mind was still trudging along logically. They had stormed a warehouse, a storage facility of some kind. It wasn't where Leviathan was receiving the Chamalla, but they had definitely used the location to store the finished product. It made natural sense to have appeared in McCarthy's search, what with the area being an industrial center; the entire facility was basically one big refinery.

But if that was the case, Brennan realized, then Bishop must have had the right location. Hope swelled in his chest as he sent a series of flashes through the wristband. *Negative position,* it told her. He felt a weight lift from his shoulders. It was disappointing that *he* hadn't been the one to finish the case, but the point of their plan had been accomplished. With both locations stormed, Leviathan was finished. He put the patch in an evidence bag and stored it in his vest pocket.

Brennan stretched his neck and heard several pops. Around him, the men were getting the message and generally putting themselves at ease. A few continued to check in and around the warehouse, but it was obvious that the place was deserted except for them. The mission was over, and night was falling. They would soon be home with their families.

He looked at his wristband again. Bishop was taking a long time to respond. He sent a prompt for acknowledgement and waited a minute with no reply. A cold feeling crept into the pit of his stomach. He pulled out his phone and dialed Bishop, subtlety be damned. It rang for half a minute and died without an answer.

He dialed again. On the fourth ring, the call was picked up.

"Bishop! Why didn't you respond?"

A male voice coughed. "Detective Brennan?"

"Yes, who is this? Why do you have Bishop's phone?"

"Taken, sir," the man said. He coughed again, and there was the sound of something wet landing on the floor. *Christ,* Brennan thought. *He's coughing up blood.*

"What happened, officer? Where is Detective Bishop?"

The response was weaker now. "They were armed, sir. The men—they're all dead. Jesus, they're all dead." His voice edged toward hysteria.

Brennan fought to control his stomach. The entire uptown squad had been wiped out. Men and women of the badge, killed, just like that. *And Bishop…*

"Taken. What do you mean, she was taken?" He heard more coughing, accompanied by more blood splattering on the floor. A loud clatter followed; Bishop's phone had fallen to the ground. "Officer—" He realized he didn't even know the man's name. "Respond!"

The men in Brennan's squad watched him with wary gazes, questions plain on their faces. Some of them wore grim masks; they had already guessed what must have happened. Brennan held the phone to his ear long enough to hear the wounded officer's final gasps.

Silence.

CHAPTER TWENTY-TWO

THE MOON WAS partway through its ascent when Jeremy walked through the front door.

In spite of his father being out of shape and Jeremy being in pain, their legs had kept moving into the night with unnatural determination. Jeremy felt the burst blisters on his feet with acute clarity, the abrasive pain announcing itself anew with each step. His father, in no better condition, managed to shamble on. Both of them were pushed well beyond the point where Jeremy would have normally called for a rest. In fact, he had tried to just sit down and stop several times, but his body had refused him. It moved of its own accord—or rather, of his uncle's accord.

The pace set by his uncle's imposed compulsion, however, meant that they moved at a much faster pace than the day before. Much of the ground had dried in the day's sun, and traveling unburdened, the two made excellent time through the thick fields and flat grasslands. Even the hills hardly slowed them down; Jeremy felt the lactic acid in his legs, and sweat poured freely from his brow, but his uncle's words had somehow given them incredible endurance.

It was only when he was stepping through the door that Jeremy realized his body was not any stronger than it used to be. His bones ached, his feet were sore, and there were more cuts on his body than he cared to think about, not to mention the dehydration that came from nonstop cross-country running. He was reaching a breaking point.

"Where have you been?" Annabelle asked as they entered. "You promised to be back hours—Oh my God!" she exclaimed. "What happened to you two?"

Jeremy looked down at himself. His outfit was tattered and torn in a dozen places; he hadn't realized how rough the terrain had been on their clothes until just now. On the exposed skin were fine lines of blood from pushing stubbornly through thorny bushes and catching himself whenever he fell. While they had been running, nothing had existed except for following Uncle Rick's order. Now, he was beginning to think clearly again, and he tried to respond to his mother. His voice croaked incoherently.

"What?" she asked.

"Water," he finally managed. His father was breathing heavily, and he either would not or *could* not talk. He blinked furiously and searched about the room with a confused look. Annabelle handed them each a tall glass of water before stepping back and folding her arms, still clearly upset but patiently waiting for Jeremy to regain his voice.

"Trip took…longer…than expected," Nathaniel gasped.

"You think?"

"Mom, we didn't mean—"

"This is so *typical* of your brother," she said to Nathaniel. "Every time he comes around, he has another harebrained scheme to involve you in. I can't believe you still go for it!" Her voice turned inward. "You know, for a second—for one brief, *shiny* freaking moment—I thought Rick had changed." The edge to her tone returned as she said, "And I thought *you* had changed. But no, I was wrong. And I am sick and tired of being disappointed by you. Jeremy, go to your room," she added absently, her eyes still on his father.

"Mom—" he started to protest.

"Room. Now." Her voice never rose and never quavered, but it was deadly in its quietness. He walked unsteadily down the hall toward his bedroom. His legs shook violently and threatened to give way beneath him; whatever his uncle had done to them, it left his body running on fumes. To emphasize that point, his stomach growled loudly, like a small bear cub.

Bear cub, Jeremy thought. His eyes widened, and he turned around abruptly. "Mom, there was a bear!"

She faced him with hands on her hips. "What are you talking about?"

"In the valley, there was a big black bear."

Annabelle looked suddenly around the room, apparently just noticing the missing member of their party. "Where is Rick?"

Nathaniel pointed toward the dark window, and Jeremy supplied the words. "Last time we saw him, he had turned to face the bear."

"On his own?"

"We…didn't really have a choice," Jeremy said. He knew now what his uncle was capable of—supported by the memories he had absorbed—but he had no idea how to broach that topic with his parents. And if he revealed that his uncle had a power, he didn't like where the resultant line of questioning would lead to.

Straight back to me.

His mother nodded and somewhat regained her composure. "I'm certain he can look after himself," she said.

"We aren't going to go look for him? We should call the cops, at least."

"I will not put you in any more danger, Jay. And the police have better things to do than tromp through the woods looking for a man and a bear. Your uncle will be fine, now go to bed."

Jeremy saw that the argument would not move any further, and trudged painfully to his room. He removed the ripped, oversized clothing. His open blisters clung to the inner lining of his boots, and the skin tore fresh as he peeled them off his feet. There was a strong, damp odor to the clothes as well; they had slept in the same gear and walked or run almost nonstop since leaving the Scott ranch. He was tempted to simply throw everything in the fire, but he settled for dropping them in the farthest corner of the room.

He donned some loose-fitting sleeping clothes and collapsed face-first into bed, his nose squished against the pillows. His brain was exhausted. He had had one hell of a long day, and when he added his uncle's memories to those of his mother and father—*on top of* those from his own life—his head felt full, heavy, and dull. He wanted nothing more at that moment than to fall asleep, but some tiny part of his brain kept moving along despite his wishes. He closed his eyes, and scenes from Uncle Rick's past came to him, unbidden.

It was a bright, sunny spring day, and the blossoming trees that lined the brick pathways of Odols University were in full bloom. Jeremy stood in front of a young, sandy-haired Nathaniel, and they were loitering outside of the admissions building. Students passed by with backpacks and books, and Jeremy was talking to his brother encouragingly.

"I guarantee that you're going to love it here," he said, patting his younger brother on the shoulder.

"You never went to college," Nathaniel argued. "Why can't I stay at home and work with you and Dad?"

Jeremy shook his head. "Mom always wanted us to go to college. At least now, she can be proud of one of us."

Nathaniel's brow furrowed the way it always did when he was upset. "She left us, though. And she left Dad."

Once again, Jeremy shook his head, but he only smiled at his brother. "One day, you'll understand," he said. "And you'll thank me for this."

"But what if—?"

"Nate, I don't want to hear any more complaints, all right?" His voice took on the deep, rich suggestive tone that he would exude continuously as a grown man. "Do well in school, be successful, and make us all proud." He gestured to the campus around them, adding, "And while you're here, if you can, find a girl you like and make her yours." His voice was joking, but Jeremy watched as his father's expression never changed.

Derrick probably never even knew what he had done that day. This was the day that had shaped his father's life—forever.

In the blink of an eye, another memory pushed its

way to the fore.

Jeremy was in a living room, though none that he had ever known. He checked his father's memories and found the answer: it was his and Annabelle's shared apartment, shortly after his own graduation. But Jeremy could see in the reflection of the mirror that the body he was in was not Nathaniel's.

Derrick's eyes reflected back at him, and he had his arms wrapped loosely around Annabelle's waist. He held her close—too close—and they were swaying back and forth in rhythm to a slow song of piano and saxophone. Annabelle's head rested against his chest, and her delicate lips were slightly tilted in a smile.

Abruptly, almost violently, Jeremy was ripped from that memory and transplanted into a living nightmare.

The air was thick and humid, and the ground he walked on was soft beneath his feet. Everything around him was vibrant and alive, and the noise of so many animals crying out at once was overwhelming. He avoided breathing when he could, and took short, shallow breaths when his lungs finally demanded air. As he looked around, Jeremy saw purple lines that coursed along tree roots and visibly spread their tendrils up the trees even as he watched.

The howling of the monkeys, the calls of the birds, and the cries of the insects nearly drove him mad, and he realized what was causing the uproar: the rainforest was dying.

Whatever they'd used to poison the air, it hadn't been

restricted to a few guerrilla rebels. Everything that breathed air and drank water was now falling to the ground in submission to death.

Jeremy woke with a start. He was back in his bedroom, and he pinched himself just to make sure it wasn't another dream. The hearth was dark, and the room felt cold without hungry orange flames licking at the blackened stone frame of the fireplace. He breathed deeply, his lungs begging for fresh air even as his brain tried to slow his rapidly beating heart. Adrenaline pumped fervently through his veins. He looked at the clock by his bed. It was the middle of the night, and he had only been sleeping for a few hours. His head ached horribly, and it felt like only moments ago that he had been closing his eyes.

Another thing became glaringly obvious to him: the reason why his father had had a doctor with him coming to the valley. It wasn't for a routine blood test; it had been for a very specific reason. And after seeing the way Ellie interacted with animals and the stark differences in their appearances, her hair dark while Jeremy's was fair, Jeremy realized that his sister was very possibly only half that. They shared a mother, certainly, but Ellie's father…Jeremy shuddered. What had Uncle Rick done to their family?

He swung his legs out over the edge of the bed and rose with purpose. He changed into fresh clothes that covered his arms and legs, mindful now of the briar patches and long fields of switchgrass that lay before him. The borrowed memories had felt like a curse ever since he'd gotten them, but now he knew the purpose of his newfound power. His uncle was dangerous—one of the seriously *bad* people that Old Ben would want him to fight. But how could he hope to stand against a man with Uncle Rick's ability, a man who could force people to bend to his will with a single word?

Jeremy glanced around the room, hoping for inspiration, when his eyes fell upon the full-length mirror that stood in the corner. He pursed his lips and nodded. *It could work.*

From one of his drawers he pulled out an old t-shirt, one he hadn't worn in years, and wrapped it around his hand. It was cinched tight with a knot he held in his closed fist. He pulled back a nervous fist and punched, but it was weak and lacked conviction. He was too scared of his knuckles being sliced open. The cloth-bound punch hit the mirror with a dull thud. The glass vibrated for a second before settling again.

Jeremy was struck with a thought, and he silently opened the door to his bedroom. The house was dead silent, and the only light to be seen was that of the moon shining in through the windows. He stepped forward on the balls of his feet, willing the floorboards not to creak beneath his weight. His sneakers—unworn since the Tower—were settled next to each other by the door. He picked them up and made a hasty retreat to his room, shutting the door behind him. He wadded up several shirts and stuffed them in the crack under the door, hoping to muffle as much sound as he could.

He faced the mirror with a shoe held aloft in one hand. Confident in his safety but worried about the noise, he struck the glass with the hard rubber heel. It vibrated more violently than before, but the surface remained unbroken. Smudged, but whole.

Frustrated, he swung harder than he meant to, and the top half of the mirror shattered beneath his shoe. He jumped away before any shards could land on his feet, which were covered only by socks. Glass smashed loudly against the floor, and Jeremy cringed as he waited for the entire house to wake up.

Miraculously, nobody came running. His rudimentary soundproofing had been enough to keep the noise from reaching the rest of the house.

He reached down, picked up a shard of glass the size of his palm, and wrapped it in cloth so that it was completely bundled up. Reasonably certain that the sharp edges wouldn't cut through the fabric, Jeremy tucked it in his back pocket and put on his sneakers. He would sweep up the rest of the broken mirror in the morning when he returned.

His stealthy retreat from the house was interrupted by footsteps approaching from the other end of the hall, and he froze as Ellie appeared in the moonlight. She was barefoot and dressed only in pajamas, but her eyes were fully alert as she looked at him skulking in the hallway.

Should he tell her what he'd uncovered? He quickly discarded the thought. Even if he *could* convince her of the memories he'd absorbed, what would it solve? There was no upside to her knowing the truth. If Uncle Rick was actually her father, it wouldn't change anything. She was still his little sister.

"Where are you going?" Ellie asked.

"What are you doing up?"

"I heard a noise and got out of bed."

"Well, go *back* to bed." He felt bad being curt, but he didn't have time to deal with her, not with the fate of their family hanging in the balance.

"Not until you tell me what is going on," she argued, literally putting her foot down with a small stomp. "Where were you and Dad all day? Where is Uncle Rick?"

"I really don't have time to explain, Ellie, please. I'm going to find Uncle Rick now, and I'll be back in the morning. I promise."

"You didn't keep your last promise."

"Neither did you," he countered. Ellie shifted on her feet, and Jeremy could have sworn he saw her blush, but it was too dark to be certain. He thought quickly. "Look, it's *really* important that you keep this one, okay?"

"Keep this one what?"

"Keep this secret," he said patiently. "You can't tell anyone where I'm going or what I'm doing, not until morning, at least. When I get back, I'll explain everything to you."

She frowned and bit her lip. "You have until eight to spill the beans."

He looked at the clock mounted behind her; it was nearly one o'clock. "Ten," he countered.

"Nine o'clock, and if you're a minute late, I'll tell Mom everything."

Jeremy grinned. "You don't know anything," he said, "but go ahead and try. I'll be back way before then."

"You promise?"

"Yes, Ellie," he sighed. "Cross my heart, blah, blah. Can I go now? We're going to wake Mom up if we talk any longer."

Ellie nodded and stepped aside to let him pass. "Be safe, big brother," she whispered, sounding more serious than he had ever heard before.

He looked at her and gave a quick smile as he

touched the bandage on his head. "I'm always safe."

She snorted, and Jeremy ducked out the front door. He started off in the direction of the Tower, taking the dirt path that was most easily visible in the moonlight.

His thoughts flashed back to the jungle memory, obviously of his uncle's time in Brazil. Everything had been dying, and he knew now that the earlier story had been a complete lie. They had taken out the drug lord, but not without also poisoning the rest of the jungle. Plants and animals had died by the thousands at the hands of one man, the very same man who felt confident in facing a grown black bear with only a small knife.

And now he was here, planning who knew what with the fate of the valley.

His uncle was the most dangerous man alive, and Jeremy had to confront him.

Chapter Twenty-Three

It was past one in the morning when Brennan finished typing his report of the failed raid on the warehouse.

By then, news of what had befallen Bishop's team had reached the rest of the precinct. They had already sent a relief squad, but the only officers returning from her squad came in body bags. Bishop herself was still missing, whereabouts unknown.

He cursed as he slammed the door to his apartment shut behind him. *I should have been there with her.* It was stupid to split up; even if they had hit the wrong place first, at least they would have known where Leviathan *was.* The door to his left creaked open, and he had his sidearm up and ready with a twitch.

"Woah, woah!" Greg said, slowly emerging from the bedroom. "Uncle Arty, it's me."

Brennan had forgotten that his nephew was staying with him. His heartbeat slowed precipitously as he lowered the gun. "I'm sorry," he said. He rubbed at the bridge of his nose. "I've—it's been a long day."

"Long week," Greg said morosely. Brennan nodded sympathetically. He shrugged out of the bulletproof vest he still wore and slung it over a chair. Greg raised an eyebrow. "They let you keep those?"

"Occupation just got a lot more dangerous," Brennan said. "We lost half a dozen good officers tonight." The words were raw on his tongue. He still couldn't believe how far south their plan had gone. *His* plan. He had never consulted Bishop on what they should do with Sam's lead; he just made a plan and ran with it.

"What happened?"

"We had a lead that went horribly wrong. And Bishop…" Brennan said, his voice trailing off. "She was taken."

Greg's eyes widened with comprehension. "Was it a theater? Did she go missing at a theater?"

"What?" Brennan looked at him, confused, until he remembered his nephew's Chamalla-induced vision. "No," he said. "It was an, uh, a factory, in uptown."

"Oh." Greg looked everywhere else in the room for a few seconds before his eyes finally fell back on Brennan. "I'm sorry. To hear that she's missing, I mean."

Brennan grunted.

"It's better than if she were dead, right?" Greg continued. "I mean, she wasn't among the dead officers, so they probably want her alive for some reason."

"What reason would that be?" Brennan snapped. He moved to tower over his nephew. "How is that supposed to make me feel better, knowing she's probably suffering somewhere? These people wouldn't spare her out of pity, or because she's a woman! No, they're going to make her miserable for every second of life she has left. She is going to die, and it won't be quick, and it will all be *my* fault!"

Greg retreated to the couch, and Brennan realized he was putting a safe distance between them. "I was only trying to help," he said. "Even if she is being tortured, that means she is still alive somewhere, and *that* means you still have a chance to find her. Are you really going to waste your time wallowing in self-pity, or are you going to rescue her?" His eyes held a flinty gaze that made Brennan look away in shame.

"You're right," he admitted. Brennan felt his anger, hot and roiling inside. Slowly, it oozed out of him like a toxic sludge, something that would only harm him if held on to. His fists unclenched, and the lines on his face became less severe. With a wearied sigh, he grabbed a Coke and joined his nephew on the couch. "We still have no idea where Bishop is being kept. Her phone was dropped during the assault, and they must have destroyed or discarded her communicator." He held up his arm in explanation, showing the black glass band wrapped around his wrist.

Greg winced. "You don't all have GPS locators embedded in your necks or something?"

"You've been reading too much science fiction," Brennan said. His gaze moved carelessly around the room as he spoke. "No, none of that, and Sam can't find her any more than the department can." His frown deepened. "There's no other—"

His eyes landed on the bulletproof vest hanging from the chair. There, poking out of one of the side pockets, was an evidence bag. Grimacing, he lifted himself from the couch, set down his Coke, and retrieved the small zipped bag from its hiding place. Inside, clearly visible through the plastic, was the single Chamalla patch from the warehouse crate.

"Is that what I think it is?" Greg asked. There was something covetous in his voice that Brennan didn't like.

"Yeah," Brennan said absently, moving to put it away again.

"No!" Greg shouted, holding up a hand.

"Just...no. Hold on," he said. "I think I know a way I can help you."

"You do?" Brennan arched an eyebrow. He followed his nephew's hungry stare to the bag in his hand. "No," he said. "Absolutely not."

"Please, Uncle Arty," he said. "I can find her."

True.

The small voice in his head rocked Brennan on his heels. That simple statement, more than anything, convinced him of his nephew's sincerity.

Brennan knew he wouldn't find another opportunity like this. There was too much going against him and not nearly enough time left for Bishop. But Chamalla was potent, even deadly. Was it worth the risk of Fracturing his nephew?

Even if he came through it safely, Brennan didn't know if he could live with that choice, if he could knowingly put his nephew in such a dangerous position. He moved ever so slightly toward the couch. "You realize what you're suggesting?" he asked. Greg nodded, his eyes never leaving the patch. "And you realize the consequences it might have?"

Greg sharply locked gazes with him. "I can find her," he repeated.

True.

Brennan sighed, and he knew his soul would be tarnished by his selfish choice. He tossed the evidence bag toward his nephew. Greg caught it a little too eagerly out of the air. Brennan watched as he ripped the patch free from its packaging and positioned it delicately over the broad side of his bicep. It sizzled slightly as it made contact with his skin, a sound that horrified Brennan, but then his nephew arched his back and he knew it was too late—the Chamalla was already working its way through his system.

When his head lowered again, his brown eyes were dull and unfocused. Greg sighed in bliss. "Ahhh, that's so good," he murmured.

Brennan pressed a fist against his forehead. "Greg," he said patiently, "I need to find Bishop."

"What? Uncle Arty, what're you...?" The question trailed off as his eyes trained on a bare spot on the wall.

"Greg!"

"Hey!" he suddenly cried. "Don't go in the theater! Uncle Arty, you need to go ahead of her! It's chivalrous!"

"I need you to focus, damn—"

Greg's eyes suddenly zeroed in on Brennan. The intensity of his stare was unnerving, but not nearly as unsettling as the slender rings of blue that surrounded his pupils like azure halos. "She's in uptown," he said, his voice eerily calm. "In the abandoned hospital."

"How do you know?" Brennan asked. A chill ran

down his spine as he kept his nephew's gaze.

"There isn't much time." Greg's head suddenly lolled, and when it bobbed up again, the blue rings had disappeared from his eyes. Whatever prescient power had been there before had evidently vanished. "There isn't much time," he repeated thickly, sounding drunk.

His heartrate soared as adrenaline surged through his veins. Brennan reached out and quickly tore away the patch from his nephew's arm; he didn't want him to be any more exposed than he already was. Still, several minutes had already passed, and there was no way of telling how much of the patch had been absorbed into his skin.

The patch squelched as it unclenched its hold on Greg's arm, and his nephew cried out in sudden pain as red, welted flesh revealed itself beneath. "Don't take it off!" he yelled, but it was too late. Brennan held the patch by the tiniest bit of its corner, a rim of unsaturated cloth that didn't hold any of the corrosive chemicals. He curled it into his pocket and hurried for the door.

Brennan couldn't waste a second. He knew where to go now, and Bishop's life hung in the balance. The bulletproof vest hugged his chest snugly. He looked over at his nephew and frowned. He didn't want to leave him here alone, but there was no time to make better arrangements. It took a moment to secure the small liquor cabinet and the bedroom door, and he left the bathroom unlocked for when Greg eventually needed to purge his body of the toxins surging inside. He locked the apartment door behind him.

As he hit the stairs, he pulled out his phone and made a call. "Yeah, Sam? I need you."

CHAPTER TWENTY-FOUR

THE FULL MOON shone on Jeremy as he made his way toward the Tower.

Pale, ghostly light gave sinister shadows to the black walnuts that inhabited the valley, and he passed Ellie's favorite pond on the way; its water was inky black in the dead of night. His feet ached and the sore muscles in his legs protested when his stride lengthened out. Still, with firm ground beneath his feet and the strong light of the pregnant moon to guide his path, he managed a solid pace. Familiarity was making the distance pass more quickly as well. He could see where their steps had sunken into the mud a day and a half ago, and when he reached the rocky outcropping, the faintest outline of the fort was visible off in the distance. It was only logical that his uncle would return to their campsite.

All the while, he kept his ears perked and his eyes open for the black bear. Crickets chirped in the night, and once or twice he was spooked by a rustling in the bushes, only to find that it was a squirrel or small skunk running from the sound of his footsteps. The whole trip, the only apparent danger he faced was the possibility of falling in the dark and injuring himself. If he was left alone out here, tired and hungry and injured, he could very easily die. His parents wouldn't notice his absence until morning, and by then it might be too late to do anything for him. The best he could do was to remain alert and move with caution. It wasn't until he was walking through one of the denser patches of trees that he realized his uncle might not even be around at all.

"If I were him," Jeremy said aloud, pushing past a stubborn branch, "I would have moved far, *far* away from here by now. And now I'm talking to myself; probably not the best indicator of my mental health."

He walked until he broke through the tree line and then collapsed to the ground. He simply lay on his back; the wrapped-up mirror in his back pocket rubbed flat against him. Unobstructed by trees, the infinite majesty of space looked down upon him. Jeremy's eyes had adjusted to the dark, and without any real light sources in the valley, he paid witness to countless stars in the sky above him.

Three thousand stars. The figure appeared in his head, and he realized it was one of Annabelle's memories resurfacing. Astrology had been one of the areas of her studies at the university. Approximately six thousand stars were visible at any time from the equator; compensating for living in either the northern or southern hemisphere, that number was halved.

"Three thousand," Jeremy murmured. It seemed like there were so many more. There were more people in his high school than there were visible stars in the sky. His mother's memory wanted to go on, to point out that some of the lights were actually galaxies that contained billions of stars. In that case, there would be—

He shook his head and curled up his legs, holding them close within his arms. There was so much he knew now, so much that had come from the memories of his parents—and now his uncle—that threatened to overwhelm him. That knowledge was too much to keep in one head. He felt it, even now, the cumulative life experience of a century and a half. Uncle Rick's memories had been the hardest to absorb because Jeremy knew—he *knew*—that each story he had told them as children was darker and truer than they had ever suspected. Absorbing all of that misery, that chaos, would surely drive him to madness. He would need to learn how to control these memories before they consumed him, especially if he wanted to become a Sleeper like Old Ben.

Before he had gained this power, whatever it was, there had been no question of where he would end up. He would have gone to Odols University, graduated with whatever degree he wanted, and then returned home to live off his father's wealth. Perhaps he would have traveled like Uncle Rick, but that was before he'd discovered the truth behind all of those stories. His uncle was not a man to be admired or copied. But Old Ben had been drawn to his power and offered him another life, one with purpose. Not a boogeyman, as the children's tales told, but a peacekeeper. A Sleeper.

But that dream could never be fulfilled if Uncle Rick was allowed to stay.

Jeremy's joints popped as he stood, and the moon watched him balefully as he began to walk. The leaves rustled as the wind blew gently through them, and keeping his mind occupied on other things made the steps pass more easily. It was a pleasantly warm summer night—*early morning*, Jeremy amended. It was easily a couple hours past midnight by now. It was the hour that ghosts walked the earth, when humans were supposedly closest to death.

His short rest break had done wonders for his body, and he hadn't realized the progress he'd made until the land started to slope gradually upward beneath his feet. His eyes glanced up and caught the distinctive rise of the fort's stone walls. Flickering orange light danced against the stone archway of the entrance.

His heartbeat sped as he crept up the ditch in front of the fort and leaned against the wall to peek around the corner.

There, seated on a hunk of rubble and tending to a small fire, was Uncle Rick.

He hunched over the little source of warmth with a haggard look, and there was a fresh cut that ran down the side of his face. His clothes were tattered, and he didn't seem to notice Jeremy as he moved closer to the edge of the fire's light. Beside him, to Jeremy's surprise, was a long, crude wooden spear. Its shaft was longer than he was tall, and the last half foot of it tapered to a deadly point. The wood of its tip was darkened, stained with blood.

Jeremy must have made some noise, a scuffle of his shoe, because his uncle suddenly rose from his seat. He turned toward Jeremy with startling speed, the rough-hewn spear gripped tightly in his calloused hands. It was half extended toward him out of sheer reflex.

He gulped. "Uncle Rick," he said quickly. "It's me, Jeremy."

"Jeremy?" his uncle whispered. "What the hell are you doing here?" He lowered the spear and brought forth a flashlight from his side. It shone brightly in Jeremy's face, which was good, because the hand he raised to shield his eyes also hid his bared teeth. Uncle Rick might have been caught off guard by the meeting, but *he* was prepared.

"I came to find you, Uncle," he said, his voice breathy. He tried to sound nonchalant, but his heart was hammering on the inside. Nearly getting run through with a spear could do that to someone. "Where is the bear?"

Uncle Rick leaned the spear against the heavy canvas tent. "We came to an understanding," he said dryly, gesturing to the equally dry stain at the pointed tip. He sat down again by the fire, affixing Jeremy with a critical eye. "You didn't have to come all this way," he continued. "I would have been home by sunrise, or maybe midday at the latest. Your dad made it home safely, too?"

"Yeah," Jeremy said. He struggled to maintain his composure, to keep any emotion from slipping into his voice. He took a step closer. "He and Mom are at home, sleeping."

"As you should be," his uncle said sternly. "What on earth were you thinking?"

"I thought I needed to come find you." Another step closer. "You worry me."

"You could have gotten lost," Uncle Rick scolded,

"or injured yourself, or there could be more dangerous animals around. I can take care of myself. You, on the other hand…what you did was reckless!" His face reddened. "I don't care how worried you were for me. And when we get home, I'm—"

"No, Uncle. I didn't say I was worried for you." Jeremy was nearly within arm's length of the spear now. *One more step.* "I said you worry me."

Confusion drained some of the color from his uncle's features. "I don't understand." He seemed to just then realize how close Jeremy had come to him, and dancing flames were reflected in his eyes. His lips curled at the edges. "If this is some kind of joke—"

"No joke," Jeremy said. His voice was utterly calm, eerily devoid of emotion. Likewise, his hand reached out and grasped the haft of his uncle's spear as if it were the most natural thing. It was rough on his palm and slightly too wide for his grip, but it would do.

"Jeremy, put that down!" Uncle Rick rose to his feet and placed the fire between the two of them. "I don't know what game you're playing at, but it needs to stop this instant! Stop it!" His voice was deep and rich, tapping into his power of persuasion.

Waves of haze-inducing command crashed against the walls of Jeremy's mind, and he fought to resist his uncle's influence. Jeremy laughed harshly. He idly caressed the tip of the spear, as if testing its point.

The bear's blood had dried, and flakes of it came off beneath his touch. "That won't work on me anymore, Uncle," he said. His eyes flashed with firelight as he looked up sharply. He was aware of the flush in his face, a heat for which the flames were not altogether to blame. He shook the spear as he spoke. "See, it took me a while, but I finally have you figured out. It all makes sense now, really. I can't believe I didn't see through you before."

"I have no idea what—"

"Do *not* lie to me!" Jeremy feinted with the spear, and his uncle took several steps back. "I've only just discovered mine, but you've had *your* power for a long time now, haven't you? Ever since you were young."

His uncle's mouth gaped a few inches, though no words came out.

"Yeah, that's what I figured. And who did you first use it on?" Jeremy checked his memory. "Oh, that's right. You told the kids who were picking on your little brother to leave him alone. You were smaller then, no bigger than any of those older kids, but they listened to you. And you wondered."

They took another step together, Jeremy advancing and his uncle retreating, the space between them always just barely wider than a lunge could carry the spear.

"You wondered, and you tried it on your parents.

Your mother was gone, so you tried it on your dad. He got his shit together, and soon you boys no longer lived in the uptown slums. It could have stopped there, but it didn't. You wanted *everything* to be the best." Jeremy broke off in a laugh that bordered on maniacal. "And you know what? I can understand that. I sympathize, I really do." Another tandem step; they were in the middle of the courtyard now, equally far away from the entrance and the Tower. "You used it on my father—your *brother*—and even *then* you meant well! Do you remember what you said to him?"

Uncle Rick's face was a mask of horror. "How do you know all of this?"

Jeremy ignored him. "You said, 'Do well in school, be successful, and make us all proud.'" The memory was fresh and crisp in his mind. He fixed a venomous glare at his uncle. "And then you added, 'Find a girl.' As an *afterthought*. And he did! He did all of that! Poor as he had been, terrified as he was of being alone, you helped him become successful and happily married." Jeremy's heart grew heavy as he lived out the emotional memories of both his mother and father. "They found love," he said quietly.

"Jeremy, I think this has gone far enough. There are some things in my past that I haven't told you, and I'm not proud of that, but if you could just put down the spear so we can talk—"

"No!" The rage and fury he had discovered in those memories boiled up inside. He gripped the spear in both hands and jabbed. "Does this look like a negotiation?!"

His uncle dodged away from the weapon's point and fell back on his hands and rear. He scrambled backward toward the main entrance of the fort.

"Your command drove my father to do great things, just like you wanted," Jeremy said. He was surprised by the strength of his own voice; if he hadn't kept his arms moving with the feinting jabs, they would have been shaking. He was at his limits, both physically and mentally. "But his work never ended, and you jumped into the void it created between him and my mother!"

"We were in love," Uncle Rick argued. His power still flowed into his voice, but the deep tones that hinted at persuasion rolled off of Jeremy, incapable of swaying him.

"She was confused, and you took advantage of it," Jeremy accused. "You still come and go as you please, and they never question it because you *make* them think it was their idea to begin with! You've come and had your time here—now I think it's time for you to go."

"Go? Please, Jeremy, think about what you're doing." He rose to his feet, snarling, uncaring of the spear pointed at his chest. "If you're going to kill me, you'll have to do it like a man."

Jeremy was dwarfed by his uncle, and he fought to hide the rush of fear he felt. If he screwed up, if his plan didn't work or his uncle resisted, he could easily be overpowered by the larger man. He gulped as he reached behind his back and grabbed the mirror that had been tucked away in his waistband. Some of the cloth had come loose, and jagged glass bit into his fingers as he gripped it.

"I want you to go," Jeremy said. He carefully held the mirror aloft, aimed at his uncle; the spear in his other hand kept his uncle from making a grab for it. Drops of blood fell from the edge of his palm as the two locked gazes. "And you're going to give the order yourself," he said, "so that you can never return."

Uncle Rick glanced between Jeremy and the mirror. "Is this really what you want? For me to go and never return?"

"Did I stutter?" His knuckles cracked as he tightened his grip on the spear. "Look straight into the mirror and give the order."

"Or what?" his uncle challenged. "You'll stab me?"

Jeremy leapt forward and bit at his uncle's thigh with the tip of the sharpened wood. Uncle Rick dodged to the side at the last second, but its point still dug a furrow in the muscly flesh there, a cut three inches long. He growled in surprise and clamped a hand over the wound.

"Don't test me," Jeremy said. More blood seeped from the fingers holding the jagged piece of mirror. "Do it. Now."

Uncle Rick gave him a stern look and then shifted his attention to the glass. "Go home," he said, his voice rich and deep. "Leave the valley and never come back. Don't bother your family ever again."

Several moments passed, and nothing happened. His feet stayed firmly planted on the ground, showing no sign of the forced compulsion that Jeremy had felt hours earlier.

A tight knot formed in his gut.

Uncle Rick advanced a step. "You see, Jeremy, I built up an immunity to this a *long* time ago. I know my own power better than anyone else alive. You're just coming into your own"—his voice became infused with an even greater level of resonating power—"but I've had decades to perfect mine. Give it up."

Jeremy buckled under the pressure that was resonating from his uncle's voice. His knees scraped hard against the ground. Trembling overtook his hands, and the mirror shard fell with a tinkling clatter. The spear remained in his grip.

"I didn't come here to cause any trouble," Uncle Rick said. "All I want to do is open up the valley for development."

"But *why*?" Jeremy asked.

Uncle Rick's eyes darted beyond him to the Tower.

An overwhelming sense of protectiveness rose up within Jeremy. That was *his* place. He didn't know what his uncle had planned for it, but he'd seen into all of Uncle Rick's past deeds, and he knew there could be no good future where that man was concerned. He would lose all control of his body in a few seconds' time.

With the little strength he had left, Jeremy lunged forward and drove the spear clumsily into his uncle's shoulder, embedding it there. As soon as the point pierced the skin, he felt the tremendous weight lift from his mind. He could move again, and he took advantage of the momentary reprieve. Jeremy spun on the spot and sprinted for the Tower as fast as he could.

His uncle screamed in pain and rage behind him, a primal roar of defiance. Jeremy ducked inside the cylindrical tower of stone and desperately wished that the enclosure had a door. There was no place to hide in the little room. Uncle Rick would be here soon, and without a weapon, Jeremy had no way to hold him off a second time.

There was only the stone table and the staircase to nowhere. The emptiness of the room was aggravating.

Light from above caught Jeremy's eye, though, and he suddenly remembered the second level of the Tower. Would Uncle Rick even be able to climb the recessed ladder?

Jeremy slipped his fingers into the grooves in the wall and started scaling his way to the second floor of the Tower. Outside, he heard an ungodly howl of pain. It sounded like Uncle Rick had managed to take out the spear.

The five windows met Jeremy as he reached the wheel spokes landing. A soft glow emanated from their edges, even though the interior landscapes were all shrouded in night. Hours had passed since he'd left the house, and Jeremy realized that the sun would be rising any minute now. Even as he watched, the windows grew brighter, their details coming into sharper relief.

If Uncle Rick looks up here, he'll see me right away.

There was only thing left to do. Taking off his shoe, Jeremy repeated the same operation he'd performed on the mirror at home. He brought his hand back and then swung hard with the rubber heel. With experience, he knew that he had to hit it as hard and as fast as he could.

The glass shattered, and solid stone lay on the other side. It felt like pieces of Jeremy were breaking as he hurried to the other spokes and smashed the next few windows. By the time he reached the fifth and final window, the sun had definitely peeked over the horizon. The snowy landscape was almost blinding with its iridescence. Jeremy knew there was something incredible going on in this Tower, that there was something at work beyond even his wildest imagination. But he couldn't risk being seen, and the magic window was just too bright. Reluctantly, he brought back his shoe and then smashed the final window to smithereens.

As the light went out and the glass fell to the floor, a snowflake the size of a thumbnail flitted into the room and landed on his nose, chilling him for a second before turning to water.

Heavy footsteps echoed up from below, and Jeremy ducked down just in time as Uncle Rick staggered into the lower chamber. His shirt was stained crimson from the wound on his shoulder, and he used the spear as a makeshift staff for support. "Come out, Jeremy. I know you're in here."

Jeremy lay flat on his stomach and only leaned over the edge far enough to keep an eye on his uncle.

Uncle Rick trudged to the stone table and checked all around it, and then he went to the pretend staircase and felt all around at the wall where a door should have been. It was clearly too dark for him to see the recessed stone ladder.

The entrance to the Tower was getting brighter,

though. With enough sunlight, Uncle Rick would put two and two together.

"Come to me," Uncle Rick said, infusing his voice with power.

A rumbling came, and the whole foundation of the Tower shook. Jeremy held on for dear life as the wheel spokes did their best to shake him off. Uncle Rick stumbled against the stone table and grasped at its edge to hold himself steady.

Stone gave way, and Jeremy went into freefall as the spoke crumbled into huge chunks and plummeted to the floor. One chunk hit Uncle Rick high on the shoulder and seemed to hit a sensitive nerve, and his body went limp.

Jeremy screamed out as he fell headlong toward the ground. His fall was stopped short, though, as the lower half of his body smashed into the hard edge of the stone table. The wind exploded from his lungs as he curled into a ball and lost consciousness.

CHAPTER TWENTY-FIVE

SAM WAS WAITING at the shuttle station when Brennan arrived.

"Christ," he said. "Brennan, you look like—no, actually, just no. Because every time I tell you how bad you look, you try and one-up yourself."

Brennan grunted. "Just when I was getting used to your candor."

Sam spared him a smile that lasted for a scant second. "What happened to Noel?" he asked soberly. Brennan filled him in on the details as they boarded the most direct shuttle going uptown. "Jesus, Arthur! When were you going to tell me this?"

"I told you just now," Brennan said. "We knew her side of the assault went south a few hours ago—"

"And you've waited this long—"

"—but we didn't have enough intel—"

244

"—to respond!" They finished at the same time, though Sam's voice was incredulous whereas Brennan had tried to sound reasoning. "Look," Brennan said, "I didn't want to keep you out of the loop any longer than I had to. But—hey, Sam, listen to me—we couldn't do anything until now. Her entire squad went down, and there was no lead on where she was taken."

"What, and now there is?" Sam faced him squarely and his eyes narrowed. "Exactly what kind of intel are you working from?"

Brennan kept his face an opaque mask. He couldn't rightly tell Sam that he had willingly drugged his nephew in exchange for a psychic vision, one that was the product of a well-known and powerful hallucinogen. When he said it in his head like that, even he couldn't believe half of it. No, he wasn't ready to reveal what Greg could do. And who knew where the conversation would lead after that? He hated lying to his friend, but it was for his own good.

"The important thing," Brennan said, forcing calm into his voice, "is that we know where she is now." He clasped a hand on Sam's shoulder. "I need you with me on this."

Sam stared resolutely out the window for a long moment. He shrugged off Brennan's hand and looked at him with reproach. "I don't appreciate having things kept from me," he said. "But yeah, I'm with you."

"Glad to hear it."

Sam leaned against the back of the seats nearest him. "So where is the police contingent on this?" he asked, looking around at the shuttle conspicuously devoid of uniforms.

Brennan shook his head. "Not enough men and too little time. Her team went down hours ago, and who knows how long she has left? Besides, we went hot and heavy last time, and you can see how that went. No, you and me—"

"You and I," Sam corrected.

Brennan gave him an even look. "Me and you," he said heavily. "See what you did? Now you don't even come first. *We* are going in dark, as quiet as we can. If we go in with dozens of men, they'll kill her and go down shooting. Or worse, use her as a bargaining chip against us. The hospital is a big place, and we don't know how many men Leviathan has inside."

"Ballpark?"

"Probably a lot of them."

"That helps. I'm glad I asked."

"This is Bishop we're talking about. Does it really matter how many of their men stand between us?"

Sam shook his head. "Move heaven and earth, right?"

Brennan grinned fiercely. "And march through hell to get there." He glanced up at the small screen that announced each station as they passed through. "This is our stop coming up," he said.

Sam read the sign as well. "It's too soon. The uptown hospital isn't until the one after."

Brennan frowned. "The shuttle station is right next to the hospital; I guarantee they'll have someone on watch there. Our best bet is to get off here and walk the rest of the way. We can try and gain access through a service entrance."

"Even if it takes longer?" Sam asked. Brennan knew how much Sam cared for Bishop, despite his wandering eye. He resisted the urge to look at his watch. Every second delayed could mean the end of Bishop's life, but there was no other way.

"We won't do Bishop any good by getting shot fresh off the shuttle," he said, just barely loud enough to be heard over the automated voice announcing their stop. "This is the way we're doing it."

φ φ φ

THE NOW DEFUNCT Odols General North Hospital was a building of enormous size, an entire city block of whitewashed stone and marble. It wasn't the tallest building, but what it lacked in height it made up for in sheer square footage. It had fallen into disrepair over the years and passed away silently as the newer, better-equipped Odols General Central opened closer to the city's center. The rights to the property stayed in government hands, though, so no new development had taken over. Most abandoned buildings fell to squatters, and the police were too occupied with more serious matters to heartlessly evict them.

In some cases, though, the open spaces attracted the likes of Leviathan, and as an officer of the law and employee of the government who owned the building, Brennan felt fully within his rights in pursuing the trespassers.

He and Sam jogged from the shuttle station and circled around the back to the medical bay, where ambulances would drop off critical patients directly. Sam jimmied the lock while Brennan stood on guard, and after a moment the two slipped inside. The corridor was long, lined with doors, and surprisingly clean. A few pieces of ceiling tile now lay on the floor, and the electricity was shut off, but neither made the hallway impossible to navigate. Sam reached for a flashlight from his belt, but Brennan stopped his arm.

"No," he whispered. "No light. If anyone is around, they'll see us coming well before we see them." In the empty hall, there was nothing to stop the light from traveling the entire length of the corridor. Sam nodded, though Brennan could just barely see the motion.

The two walked as quietly as they could with weapons drawn. They kept their sidearms holstered; even with a silencer, pistols were noisy as hell, and it would only take one fired shot to attract every Leviathug in the building. Brennan extended one hand and let his fingertips brush along the wall for guidance, while in the other hand he held a short double-edged knife. Sam carried a hunting knife, the kind that woodsmen might use. The toothed edge opposite the blade doubled as a saw for cutting through small branches.

Brennan reached a corner and motioned for Sam to pause. He wouldn't see the curled fist that raised by reflex, but he would hear the stop in Brennan's footsteps. Tentatively, Brennan peeked around the corner. He couldn't see anybody in the pale gray of the darkened hall.

"Come," he breathed, and the two moved onward. They reached a lobby with a large double staircase; one set led to the second floor, while the other set descended into the basement of the hospital.

"Even odds in both directions," Sam said. His voice barely carried to Brennan's ear.

Brennan agreed. "Fifty-fifty." There was safety in numbers, but it would also slow down their search effort by half. "Split up," he suggested. "You go high, I'll go low."

Sam grunted affirmatively. "Heaven and hell," he said. "Good hunting."

Brennan descended the stairs without another word. He made it no more than a dozen steps before someone rounded the corner just an arm's reach away.

Reflex and training brought his knife arm swinging, and the blade plunged noiselessly into the man's neck, slicing through the jugular. He clamped his free hand over the man's mouth and moved with his body, gently easing the fall so that neither his gun nor body made a sound as they met the ground. Blood continued to pour as he slid the knife out and wiped it against the man's jacket. The dead man had a semiautomatic rifle slung across his chest, but he was otherwise unarmed and unarmored. Brennan wiped the blood from his hands as well as he could.

Thirty seconds on his own and already he had run into trouble. Brennan hoped that Sam was still hidden, still safe. He took a deep breath to slow his hammering heart and then continued. His eyes had adjusted to the dark, and he could see everything relatively clearly in differing shades of black. He stalked through the empty hall, sweeping his gaze left and right with each door.

Every room he searched was eerily empty; he had grown so accustomed to hospitals being *full*—of gurneys, nurses, whirring machines, men in white coats, visiting families, pictures, paintings, binders full of papers—that the opposite was intensely unnerving. The pervasive emptiness of the building shook him more than anything.

One long room finally showed promise. The door creaked loudly on its hinges, and Brennan cringed; he forced it all the way open with a sharp but short burst of sound. He checked the room for more members of Leviathan, but there was no movement except for the low ripple of fluid in the two basins in the room.

Each container was the size of a refrigerator on its side and twice as tall. They were laid end to end, and there the similarities ended. One held a clear substance, and one whiff of it was enough to tell Brennan that it was bleach.

The second basin held some kind of dark liquid with the thick consistency of cold maple syrup. He didn't take the risk of smelling it; it didn't take a scientist to recognize the sickly, toxic odor of Chamalla.

He retreated slowly from the room, past the syrupy hallucinogen and then past the basin of bleach that purified the patches before they were infused with Chamalla. He left the door open as he ducked back into the hallway, silent as a phantom.

He took a pair of steps around another corner before his eyes were suddenly flooded with light.

Something very, very solid smashed into him, connecting with the back of his head just below the ears.

Brennan didn't pass out, but the temporary stars in his vision and disorientation were enough to make him lose track of time as a pair of strong arms wrapped under his armpits and dragged him.

He wasn't carried for long, though, and he hit the floor hard when he was deposited. His arms felt like lead pipes; the same strong person who carried him grabbed those pipes and tightened a coarse loop of rope around his wrists, binding them behind his back. Even if he could have moved, he doubted he'd have the strength or mobility to break free.

His blurry vision cleared, and he looked dizzily around the room. It was barren, just another former patient's room. Drab wallpaper peeled on the walls, and the joined bathroom was a small husk of a room without the plumbing fixtures. Hinges squealed as the door opened, and Brennan's head snapped around to see a familiar figure stepping into the room.

It had been a while since they had seen each other, but the man still had the same college cap he had worn during their first encounter outside of Nettle's pharmacy.

"Badgercap," Brennan muttered. The word came out thick and slurred.

The man known as Badgercap carried a light into the room with him, which he held aloft as he leered at the captive detective. "Oho, oho, this is my lucky day, isn't it?" he tittered. The light jittered in his grasp, and his eyes were glazed over. A lazy smile hung on his face, which twisted with scorn as he looked at Brennan. "Another detective to start off today's body count. I had quite the success yesterday, but today is a new day, I suppose."

"You're high," Brennan said absently. Even through bleary eyes, he could see a patch on the drug lord's exposed forearm.

Badgercap opened his mouth to speak, but just then Sam appeared from around the corner, carried by the hem of his shirt. He was in the grip of a large, heavily muscled man, and his hands were bound in the same way as Brennan's. The mountain man had a massive revolver secured in a custom shoulder holster. Muscles threw Sam bodily, and he slammed against the wall beside Brennan. The sound of his body hitting brick was thick and dull, and the air rushed out of him as he slumped to the floor.

"Found this one skulking around upstairs," Muscles explained to Badgercap. His voice was a strangled growl, and the tendons in his neck were tight against his skin. "He took down two of our lookouts before I found him."

Badgercap turned and looked at Sam with a hungry smile. "Did he now?" He waved a dismissive hand toward Muscles. "Stand guard outside. There may be more than the two of them."

Muscles grunted and lumbered out of the room, firmly shutting the door behind him.

Sam seemed to be collecting his wits and lurched into a kneeling position. Badgercap moved forward and savagely kicked him onto his side.

"Stay down, dog!" he cried, adding another vicious boot to the groin. Sam's eyes screwed up in pain as he contorted, twisting his body to better protect himself.

"Hey!" Brennan shouted. "Leave him alone!" He received a swift strike to the head in response, but he rolled with the lazy blow and kept Badgercap's focus on him. "What? That all you got?"

Badgercap's smile twisted into a malicious snarl, and his eyes danced with manic fervor. "You are becoming a nuisance," he said. His voice was high and crazed, and he swung another fist that caught Brennan on the ridge over one eye. A thin line opened where he struck, and a sheet of blood began to pour down his face. "I thought my last message was clear, but apparently you need a reminder. Stay out of things that are none of your business!"

Before he could turn around toward Sam,

Brennan head-butted him at the knees. There was no real power behind the attack, but hurting him wasn't the intention. "When you killed good men and women and kidnapped my partner, you made all of this my business."

With a haughty demeanor, Badgercap gathered himself up. "You could have stopped at 'killed good men and women'," he said, breaking off into a fit of giggles. As the madman paced about and leered at them with unrestrained excitement, Brennan and Sam shared a glance.

"What do you mean?" Sam demanded, anger rising in his voice. "What did you do to Noel?"

"Me?" the maniac giggled. "*I* didn't do anything! But your partner didn't look too good last time I saw her."

True.

Sam struggled against his injured body as he rose to his feet. His lip was cracked, several fingers bent at unnatural angles, and he moved with the signs of dozens of untold injuries. His face was a mask of pure fury, and the glare he gave Badgercap made Brennan's hairs stand on end.

"If you touched one hair on her head," he growled, "I swear to God I'll—"

Badgercap produced a handgun from his waistband and shot Sam twice in the chest.

Brennan watched in horror as his best friend of over a dozen years recoiled from the shots. Sam's eyes dulled as he fell to his knees, and momentum carried his limp body to the side. He couldn't see his friend's face from where he knelt, but Brennan felt his body begin to shake as Sam lay there, unmoving. The two gunshots in the small, confined room were deafening, but they were nothing compared to the roar of rage that tore its way from Brennan's throat, a wordless howl of noise and fury.

He had murder in his heart. He had killed before in self-defense, or in the cause of protecting others, and he had never shied away from that fact. But here, now, he bore a personal hatred for the man who stood before him. Bloodied, bound, and beaten, he didn't have a snowball's chance in hell of winning. It didn't matter. He had lost two of his closest friends to this madman, and he would give everything for the chance to make him pay. Blood pumped furiously through his veins and it still came down in sheets over his face. He saw red as he rose to charge the man.

With almost casual arrogance, Badgercap turned and cracked Brennan square in the jaw with the butt of his gun. He heard the pop of a dislocated jaw as mind-numbing pain jolted through his skull. His head snapped to the side, nearly splitting itself open on the wall, and he lacked the strength to turn his face back toward his attacker.

"Now," Badgercap said, kneeling before him. He cupped Brennan's chin forcefully, the grip agonizingly painful. "Listen when you are being spoken to," he commanded. "I am Leviathan! You are nothing!" He released Brennan and stepped away sharply, pacing anxiously. His stare never left Brennan's face, and after a moment he stopped, his mouth parting slightly as if struck by inspiration.

"This should be fun," he said, his teeth gleaming, "and you don't look like you're having fun. So let's make this a bit of a game, eh? I'm a generous man, and you've got nothing left to live for, do you?" He leaned in close, and his rancid breath was warm and moist against Brennan's face. "Here's the game," he said. "You get to ask me questions, finish your investigation, and maybe die content." He lifted the pistol before Brennan's eyes so he couldn't avoid seeing it. "But for each *boring* question you ask, I get a whack at that ugly mug of yours. How long d'you think you'll last?"

Brennan spat in Badgercap's face. The other man wiped at the spit slowly, still showing his manic grin. He tried to think of an escape, a way out of this situation alive, but those options didn't present themselves. He could charge Badgercap, though that would only reward him with a bullet to the head. Likewise, he gained nothing by refusing to play his game and staying silent; if anything, that would only infuriate his captor and bring death all the more swiftly.

Though a quick death might be better.

Brennan sighed. "Zachariah Nettle," he said slowly, his jaw stiff. "You killed him."

Badgercap's eyes danced madly. "Is that a question?"

"Are you responsible for the murder of Zachariah Nettle?"

"There, that's much better now. You aren't as thick as your skull suggests." He paced slowly, holding the pistol delicately in his hands. "Yes, I killed the pharmacist. We had a good thing going until he tried to haggle with me. With *me*, the thankless wretch. He wanted a larger cut, so I agreed." His lips parted in a grisly grin. "Oh, yes, I gave him a *very* large cut," he said, pantomiming a knife slicing through the air.

Brennan felt the truth of his words. A madman he might be, but he was being honest—he was following the rules of this ghastly game. His brain worked furiously to come up with another question, but one left his lips unbidden while he thought.

"You aren't a thug," his mouth said. "The night you jumped me outside the pharmacy, you talked like a street urchin. When you just spoke now, though, that accent was gone. It was just a mask," Brennan said, meeting Badgercap's glare. "Who are you?"

"Boring!" Badgercap declared. "I'm not interested in talking about myself."

He hit Brennan with a fast left hook that stunned him more than it hurt him. Badgercap shook his hand after the punch, wincing, and then slammed the butt of the gun in his other hand in a backhanded strike to Brennan's jaw. Rather than a pop, Brennan felt something in his jaw crack. Badgercap stooped to grab him roughly by the collar of his shirt and pulled him close, speaking into Brennan's ear.

"Do not think for a second that I will hesitate to kill you. I thought I proved that with your friend here. I don't want to kill you right off because, frankly, you have been a huge pain in my ass. It is going to take *months* to put my network back together, not to mention the sales I'll lose in the meantime—No, no, this is not going to end quickly for you," he whispered harshly. "I am going to prolong your suffering for as long as I can, just like your partner. And I will enjoy every second of it."

Brennan's mind was foggy, and he was having trouble thinking clearly even as alarm bells went off in his head. He and Sam had been too late—Noel was lost even before they entered the building. Sam had paid for it with his life, and it looked like Brennan was destined to go the same way. He needed to buy more time to think of some clever escape.

"Okay, okay," he gasped, slumping to the floor as Badgercap's grip eased. His voice slurred, and it hurt to speak through his fractured jaw. "I have a quethtion," he mumbled.

Badgercap grinned, fierce and sudden, and danced back toward the door. "Well, go on, athk away!" he said excitedly, mocking Brennan's lisp as he broke down in another burst of demented laughter.

Brennan gave him a bleary glare and hoped he looked more intimidating than he felt. Kneeling on the floor with his hands bound behind his back, he didn't like the chances of that. He heard a low noise from the hallway, likely Muscles coughing.

"Why did you do it?" he asked, thankful there were no soft consonants in the question. His voice cracked with the words. "Why did you take Bishop?"

Badgercap leaned in very suddenly, smacking Brennan across the face. *No, not smacking*, he realized. In his excitement, Badgercap's motion turned the gentle swipe into a partial slap.

"Are you crying?" he asked incredulously. "Oh, but this is delicious! But I don't have an answer for you, Detective. See, I've already grown tired of our game. Your questions aren't as interesting as I'd hoped they would be." He cocked the gun and pressed it against Brennan's skull. "I hope you got the answers you were looking for."

A shot rang out, and Brennan's face became a gory mess of blood. Badgercap's chest exploded outward as a second round worked its way through his body, and he fell limply to the floor with a stunned look on his face. Behind him, leaning heavily against the open doorframe and holding Muscles' enormous revolver, was a haggard and injured Detective Bishop.

"Brennan!" she cried, dropping the gun and rushing to his side. "Oh my God, what are you doing here?"

"What am I—what are *you* doing here? I thought you were dead!"

Bishop untied the rope that bound Brennan's hands and he pulled them free, flexing them with newfound freedom. "Reports of my death," she muttered.

Brennan pointed to Sam. "He'th not bleething," he said.

"Oh God! What the hell were you two thinking?!" She rushed to Sam's side and rolled him over. His eyes were closed, and his face was starting to turn blue. "Oh God, oh God" Bishop half muttered, half prayed. Tears welled in her eyes as she crouched over Sam, her hands spreading over his chest as she leaned against his body. "What the—?" she started. "He's not bleeding."

"That'th what I thaid."

She ripped apart his shirt so the buttons flew all

across the room. Beneath his clothing was a thick, black vest. Two shiny bullets were embedded in the thick material over his heart and lungs, and Bishop tore at the Velcro straps, ripping the confining vest from Sam's body.

With an enormous gasp of breath, he sat up and looked wildly around the room.

Brennan looked at him in disbelief. "Welcome back to the land of the living," he said, still not believing his eyes. "How did you—?"

Sam coughed and gripped his chest as he struggled to catch his breath. "Sweet Jesus, that was close. How long was I out?"

"About three minutth," Brennan said.

"Is that all?" He sounded disappointed. "Well, I must've gotten CPR," he said mildly. Sam looked hesitantly at Brennan, whose face was a bruised pulp of flesh with a dead man's blood still freshly dripping from his chin, and then looked hopefully to Bishop. "Noel, *please* tell me it wasn't him." In that moment, he seemed to notice Bishop crouched next to him for the first time. "Noel!" he cried, wrapping his arms around her in a sudden embrace. "You're alive! Oh, thank God."

She accepted the hug with reluctance, though a wan smile touched her lips.

Sam looked at Brennan with shining eyes. "Your

voice sounds ridiculous, by the way. So you saved her? How'd you accomplish that?"

Bishop looked suspiciously between the two of them, and Brennan gave her a guilty grimace.

"You two were on a *rescue* mission?" she asked. Her tone took a sharp turn for the worse. "What, you think I'm some damned damsel in distress?"

"It'th nothing like that—" Brennan started, but she overrode him.

"Don't feed me bullshit, Arthur! I have been on my own here for hours," she said, speaking slowly for his benefit. "*Hours*, Brennan. Do you understand? I had plenty of time to work my way out without your help. You had no way of knowing where I was, so I sure as Hell wasn't waiting for—" She broke off suddenly, turning her glare slowly toward Sam. "Were you in on this?"

Sam held up both hands. "Completely his idea," he said, pointing to Brennan. "He just said you were in trouble, and I hopped to. When he told me to bring my gun, I figured the vest would be prudent."

"It'th true," Brennan added. "Trutht me, I'd know."

Bishop looked between the two of them, seeming mollified. "Well, thanks. Even though I ended up saving *you*." She cocked her head. "How did you know where to find me?"

Brennan waved off the question; that was getting into dangerous territory. "Another time," he promised. He winced as he stood, his legs slow to respond to his orders. "And you're welcome."

"This is all very touching," Sam drawled, "but I think now's the point where I could really use a hospital. A real hospital," he added, glancing at the rundown room they were in.

Bishop smiled in spite of herself, and she offered Sam a hand up off the floor. "Come on, you lugs. Let's get you cleaned up," she said. She looked sideways at Brennan and grimaced. "You look terrible."

"One day," he said, "thomeone will apprethiate me for more than my lookth."

CHAPTER TWENTY-SIX

JEREMY'S EYES FLUTTERED open and he looked up into the face of the man who had betrayed his family.

He gasped out for breath, but he couldn't get as much air as he needed. His lungs were seizing, and he reached out desperately to his uncle for help. But his arms refused to move with no oxygen to burn.

He wanted to hate his uncle for everything he had done. Because of Uncle Rick, his father was driven toward obsession with his work. He had nearly destroyed his parents' love for each other, and now he was here again for more unknown reasons. It didn't matter what he was here to do.

"Uncle," he said, his voice barely a whisper.

Derrick leaned over Jeremy until they were mouth-to-ear. "Jeremy, just stay with me," he said. "I'm going to get you help, you won't die here."

Die? Jeremy thought blearily. He must have been in worse shape than he'd realized.

He heard the sound of Velcro unstrapping, and Uncle Rick muttered a curse. "No cell signal. Should've figured. Don't worry, Jeremy, we'll get you some help."

"How?" he rasped. It felt like his body was made of lead.

Uncle Rick frowned down at him. He took a deep breath—a spike of envy coursed through Jeremy as he stared up breathlessly—and then he started speaking. "Jeremy, stand up. Do it now."

His words were laced with power, and for once, Jeremy didn't fight the sensation as it inundated him. His arms, which had been dead to the world just a moment before, pushed against the floor as his legs gathered up beneath him. It was an ungainly rise to his feet; he felt like a reanimated corpse freshly brought from the grave.

Jeremy's mind raced with the implications. He was completely under his uncle's spell. If he let another one of those whispered words worm its way into his brain, he would be powerless to stop whatever his uncle had planned. And if he died on the way home, what would his family believe? Surely they'd know that it was his uncle who'd killed him.

Unless he simply convinces them otherwise, whispered a small voice in his head.

266

Uncle Rick moved in to help Jeremy stand, and that was when he made his move. Jeremy lurched forward—he was too weak to do anything else—and wrapped his arms around his uncle's neck. Uncle Rick, taking it as either a gesture of affection or a plea for support, caught him and held him steady.

Jeremy planted his hands on either side of his uncle's head and forced his way into his mind. It felt like he was fighting a waterfall, the sheer immensity of it beating him back. He had no idea what to do, what to expect of this, but he had to do something. He forged ahead, exerting his will, and then like the popping of a balloon, the world changed.

Instantly, he was consumed by a rolling fog that seemed to dominate the landscape. It was not unlike the rainforest in Brazil. Large, leafy trees crowded each other for light. Thick, ropy vines climbed their way up the trunks and connected with neighboring trees. On the ground, red and brown mushrooms proliferated, each the size of Jeremy's head. Small beams of gold and bronze were visible *beneath* the soil, and they seemed to run everywhere and connect with everything.

And absolutely every living thing was infected.

Sickly purple tendrils pulsed along the trees and mushrooms like an encroaching disease. The leaves of the trees were wilted already, and the vines that hung from them lacked the vibrancy of life. Jeremy reached out a hand and touched one of the nearby trees. He recoiled from the wave of nausea that rolled over him, but he gained the insight he needed. Each one of the trees, every sickly mushroom and flower that bloomed in the landscape of his uncle's mind, was a memory. What's more, they were all slowly being infected by the very thing he had come to remove.

"What are you doing?" His uncle's booming voice seemed to come from everywhere at once.

Jeremy ignored it, and instead concentrated on the memory he wanted. Motes of amber light collected in one of the lines beneath his feet, and a moment later a burst of gold shot forward. He hurried after it, following it along a path through the damp, dark forest.

A minute in, a log tripped up his footing and he lost sight of the beam for a moment. Panic rose in his chest as he glanced about, but it was nowhere to be seen. He took off at a run, and a moment later a path opened up to his right; the beam had turned a corner around a wide and particularly sickly tree, and its golden light pulsed again as he reached it.

"The phantom memories," Jeremy said, not bothering to raise his voice. "There were moments in my parents' past that I couldn't see. You ordered them to forget, didn't you?"

The earth trembled beneath him, and Jeremy realized his uncle was shaking with dark laughter in the real world. "I knew the moment I saw that note on your desk that there was something about you," the ground roared.

"So it was you," Jeremy mumbled. He noticed with impending dread that it was hard to catch his breath, even though, technically speaking, he had no lungs here. His body was steadily failing him in the physical realm, and Jeremy realized that his uncle was attempting to stall him with all the talking. "It's not important," he said, stepping forward. "Just tying up loose ends, before *the* end."

As he navigated over fallen branches and small streams that ran along the forest's floor, he saw more and more ghastly tendrils. They became so numerous that, more often than not, entire plants appeared purple by nature.

"It needn't end like this," came his uncle's voice, issuing forth from the streams and damp undergrowth. "I could command you not to die." The trees swayed where they stood, as if they were rooted on the shoulders of a shrugging giant. "Who knows if it would work, but what is the alternative? You're dying, Jeremy."

His hairs raised on end and his stomach did a backflip. It occurred to him that his uncle *wasn't* keeping his body alive while all of this happened. Time was now his biggest enemy.

If what his uncle offered was true—was even *possible*—would it be worth the trade? He would live to fight another day, and he could confront his uncle on more even ground. Perhaps there was even something in his memories that could be used against him.

The beam of light stopped, and it pulsed consistently beneath a single mushroom the size of a beach ball. It was a solid, angry violet, and it was undoubtedly the source of the corruption that had taken over his uncle's mind.

It was the memory of his power.

Jeremy placed a hand on its crown and was overcome with revulsion. The thing *exuded* evil. He recoiled and clutched his hand close to his chest.

Is this kind of thing inside of me? The thought horrified him. His own power had come to him suddenly, and without instructions, but Old Ben had told him it could be used for good. If he kept using his power, if he kept absorbing the memories of others…would he be corrupted just as his uncle had been?

Would he become the very monster he was trying to stop?

Suddenly, he didn't feel too anxious about dying.

Jeremy steeled himself and crouched beside the enormous mushroom. He wrapped his arms tightly around its base, gritting his teeth against the waves of nausea that hit him, and he lifted up with his legs. The mushroom squished in his grip and noxious ooze slid out from its pores, but otherwise it remained firmly rooted.

The wind rose to a deafening howl and the earth shook violently beneath his feet. Uncle Rick was trying with all his might to expel him from his mind. Jeremy knew his body had little strength left.

He tugged harder, and the ground beneath the mushroom broke unevenly. Tendrils as thick as his arm connected like roots to the nearest mushrooms, and Jeremy realized that there was no way to lift it out by sheer force, not the entire system. He started kicking viciously at its stem, and bits of it gave way. He gripped a nearby rock and started using it like a crude axe against the mushroom. More of its base broke away.

Jeremy felt a strange beat inside of him, and he realized it was his own thready pulse. His body was weakening, getting ready to relinquish its hold on the world; he worked all the harder because of it. He had never attempted to *remove* a memory before, and the possibility had only come into his mind just a few minutes ago. But if it was his last act on earth, he would take his uncle's power away.

The rock tore through chunks at a time, and finally Jeremy felt that it was weak enough to try again. He braced himself, gripped under the mushroom's hood, and heaved. More tendrils broke, but not all of them. His body was in its death throes.

Jeremy was out of breath. His mind was fuzzy and his whole body clamored for him to sit down, to rest. He had done enough.

He snarled in defiance and pulled, again and again. More roots snapped each time, and he felt it giving way. The world inside his uncle's mind roared like an oncoming tide; everything was connected now to the power he was taking.

Memories flashed before his eyes, and it took him a moment to recognize them as his own. His mother, beaming at him as she returned with a bushel of freshly picked food. His father, brooding solemnly by the fireplace while he recovered from the Tower. Ellie— sweet Ellie—running carefree through the garden with her squirrel friends in tow. He wouldn't be able to keep his promise to her.

The mushroom—and the memory of power that it contained—broke free.

Then he was gone.

Epilogue

Brennan tightened his somber black tie and flattened the collar of his dress shirt.

His jaw had been set, and scans showed only a hairline fracture in the bone. No surgery required, but his face was still far from a pretty sight. The bruises had started to fade over the past few days, but they were still clearly visible in patches all over his face. At least he could pronounce soft syllables correctly again.

Greg sat on the couch with a bouquet of flowers, an untouched glass of water resting nearby. He was already suited up and ready to go, and the shakes that had accompanied his withdrawal from the patch subsided yesterday. He looked healthier, but he hadn't said a word all morning, and Brennan knew he was still hurting inside.

They were getting ready in Bishop's apartment.

She had been acting as de facto caretaker for Brennan and Sam after they were cleared from the hospital, though the latter had recovered much more quickly. Sam sat on a bar stool beside the kitchen counter. He was staring into the middle ground, keeping the entire room in view with unfocused eyes and a neutral expression on his face. He was respectfully quiet, knowing what today meant for Brennan and his nephew.

The door to Bishop's bedroom cracked open, and an orange tabby cat sprinted out into the living room. Brennan raised an eyebrow at the furry intrusion. Bishop was half a step behind it, and she delicately scooped up the cat before it could jump on Greg's lap. She held it at arm's length, not wanting to get any fur on her clothes, and she dropped it back inside her bedroom before swiftly closing the door again.

Bishop wore a black dress with a dark jacket over top, and she went without any jewelry. She wore enough makeup to hide her injuries as best as was possible. Her eyes met Brennan's briefly and she nodded sympathetically.

"Was that...?"

"Nettle's cat?" Bishop nodded. "I couldn't leave the poor thing to starve."

"Careful," Brennan said, thinking back to the yowling he'd heard earlier in the week. "She might be pregnant."

"He's a boy."

"That significantly lowers the odds, then," Sam noted.

Brennan gave them both a brief smile before the solemnity of the day brought his mouth back into a frown. He grabbed his jacket from the back of a chair and shrugged it on, smoothing out the wrinkles in front of the mirror. The four of them left in silence.

It was a short drive to the cathedral of St. Agabus, located on the western edge of the city. Nestled within one of the more affluent quarters of Odols, it was the only church Brennan knew of that served mass every day of the week. The stained-glass windows of its sanctuary were aligned with the rising and setting sun, and it was the largest cathedral in the Midwest. It was also where Brennan's family was buried.

They followed the side path that led around to the back of the cathedral. A field of standing stones rose to greet them, each one a marker for the dead. The memorials ranged from unadorned headstones in simple plots to one squat, very ornate mausoleum in the back corner. Some of the graves were adorned with recent tokens of love from visiting family members: pictures, flowers, or trinkets that carried some special meaning.

The ceremony for Madison Warner was simple

and straightforward, just as she would have wanted it to be. An older priest presided over the burial, sprinkling holy water on the casket as a thurible swung on its chain from his other hand, wafting incense over the grave. Finally, he petitioned to God that her soul should rest in peace.

No other words were spoken, and no other words were needed.

Greg stepped forward and placed the bouquet on top of the casket, over his mother's hands. His shoulders trembled, and he couldn't stop fresh tears from streaking down his face.

Brennan held him close as her body was lowered into the grave.

Goodbye.

The four of them stood around the grave for a while after the priest had departed. Time passed— minutes or hours, it didn't matter. Sam and Bishop stood in solidarity with them, for which Brennan couldn't express his gratitude enough. They were better friends than he deserved. When they were finally ready, they left the same way they had come, taking the path around the side of the massive cathedral to the parking lot.

The sky was a clear one that day, and the morning sunlight was shining directly into Brennan's eyes as they approached, but he could make out a figure standing idly by Bishop's car. He shielded his eyes with a hand and made out more features; an old-fashioned dark suit, sparse white hair, and small, dark glasses. He was small in stature, barely taller than the car he leaned against.

"Arthur Brennan," the man rasped. "We need to talk."

Bishop cast a glance between Brennan and the newcomer. "Brennan, who is this?"

"Benjamin," he growled.

His response was terse, and Bishop must have recognized the tension that suddenly settled in Brennan's shoulders. She took a half-step to the side and turned slightly, presenting a slimmer profile. Sam mirrored her movements on Brennan's other side, his eyes never leaving the strange old man.

Benjamin sighed, a sad sound coming from the frail old man, like the last bit of air fleeing a deflated balloon. "Whatever your feelings toward me may be," he said, "I am afraid you must put them aside. We have larger issues that must be dealt with."

Brennan's hands clenched into white-knuckled fists. "Any business we had together ended long ago. You have no right to be here!"

"Ah. The death of your sister is regrettable, and you have my condolences," Benjamin said lightly. "I only need a moment of your time, to convince you of my—"

"No," Brennan cut him off. "I don't want to hear it. Bishop, start the car."

Bishop unlocked the car doors with the fob in her hand. Benjamin stepped aside carefully, testing his cane against the ground before shifting his weight. Sam and Greg exchanged a glance before walking toward the car, keeping a wary distance between themselves and the strange man as they piled into the backseat. Brennan made a move toward the passenger side, but he was stopped by the wrinkled hand that shot out and grasped his arm.

"Detective," the old man croaked. "You have your reasons for disliking me. But trust me in this: death is coming to Odols."

Brennan shook off the old man's hand and put the car between them. The vehicle shifted beneath his weight as he sat down. "Bishop, we're leaving," he called before resolutely slamming the door. She joined them a moment later, her face a blank mask, and pressed a button to bring the car to life. They pulled out of the parking lot in silence.

Brennan watched her repress a shudder as they put the church in their rearview mirror. He knew all too well what thoughts were crossing through her head, since the same fear had taken hold in his own mind. Doubly so, for his power confirmed the truth of

Benjamin's words.

Death was coming to Odols.

ABOUT THE AUTHOR

What Tom wants you to know:

TOM SHUTT WRITES paranormal suspense with generous helpings of humor and a sprig of mystery thrown in for good measure. Sometimes he dabbles in fantasy, but in all cases, he strives to push the boundaries of modern fiction in search of good answers to hard questions.

He lives on the perpetually rainy East Coast with some cats, dogs, and a basement full of mistresses. His favorite authors are Jim Butcher, George R. R. Martin, Jonathan Stroud, and Eoin Colfer. He knows how to hide a body from the police, and the research for his novels has likely landed him on a few security watch lists. He enjoys reading, gaming (*Halo, Civilization, BioShock, Call of Duty, Minecraft*), playing pool, chasing deer, hunting deer, riding deer, and lying about what activities he does with deer. His favorite shows include *Supernatural, Game of Thrones, iZombie,* and anything created by Joss Whedon.

What Tom's family wants you to know:

TOM LIVED WITH more clarity, passion and dedication than most of us can ever hope to achieve in an entire lifetime, let alone just 25 years. He was hilarious, wise, thoughtful and loving. While he's left us behind physically, he's also left behind a collection of written works to keep us connected to him until we meet again. Until that day comes, we will miss him every moment.